the two doors of heaven

john bolin

the two doors of heaven

a story of your future

Multnomah® Publishers, *Sisters, Oregon*

THE TWO DOORS OF HEAVEN
published by Multnomah Publishers, Inc.
© 2005 by John J. Bolin

International Standard Book Number: 1-59052-264-8

Cover design by David Carlson Design
Cover image by Scott Gilchrist/Masterfile
Interior design and typeset by Katherine Lloyd, The DESK

The Scripture quotation in the chapter entitled "Millie" is from
John 3:16 in *The Holy Bible*, King James Version. The Scripture
quotation in the chapter entitled "On the Spot" is from John 14:6
in *The Holy Bible*, New Living Translation (NLT), © 1996. Used by
permission of Tyndale House Publishers, Inc. All rights reserved.

Multnomah is a trademark of Multnomah Publishers, Inc.,
and is registered in the U.S. Patent and Trademark Office.
The colophon is a trademark of Multnomah Publishers, Inc.

For information:
MULTNOMAH PUBLISHERS, INC.
POST OFFICE BOX 1720 • SISTERS, OREGON 97759

Library of Congress Cataloging-in-Publication Data

Bolin, John, 1969-
The two doors of heaven / John Bolin.
    p. cm.
    ISBN 1-59052-264-8
    I. Title.
PS3602.O6535T89 2005
813'.6--dc22   2004025300

05 06 07 08 09 10—10 9 8 7 6 5 4 3 2 1 0

Contents

Part I—To the Doors

Part II—Looking Through

part I

—

To the Doors

Lunch Break

‖≡

J ack Gates should have known something was about to happen. His morning had felt so strange. Something about it seemed different, almost distant, like scenes played in slow motion.

Anxious to get his blood moving again, he shifted uneasily in the cheap swivel chair and glanced around the hotel conference room—a room that was feeling smaller by the minute. *Is everyone here as zoned out as I am?* He studied a few of the forty or so faces lit by the big-screen video in front of them. Amazingly, they were still paying attention, and some were even scribbling notes. *Incredible,* Jack thought.

He had been sitting for hours at the seminar on professional and personal fulfillment. Twisting his wrist toward the light of the screen, he glanced at his watch, a Tag Heuer rip-off. 11:48. Twelve minutes till lunch. An eternity.

He stared again at the PowerPoint statements on the screen, leaned back, exhaled, and slipped both hands in his pants pockets. In one of them, he felt a piece of paper. He pulled it out—for the third or fourth time this morning—and discreetly set it beside his yellow pad on the table in front of him. Folded, it looked like a creased twenty-dollar bill. But when you opened it, you discovered it was some sort of religious tract—a trick designed to make you pick it up.

It had worked well enough on him. Hurrying to the seminar room this morning, Jack had turned a corner and seen it lying on the hallway floor. Just as he reached down and grabbed it, he heard others approaching behind him, and he was too embarrassed to drop it after seeing what it really was.

In the room's dim light, he squinted to read again the first line inside:

If you died today, do you know for sure you would go to Heaven?

He hadn't bothered reading the rest. Nor had he framed any answer to the question, except to wonder for a fleeting moment how anybody could respond to such a thing in any reasonable and objective way.

Heaven?

He was hungry. 11:51. Where should he go for lunch?

The seminar leader clicked faster through a few more PowerPoint slides. Bringing his presentation to a climax, he turned to the group, folded his arms, and asked, "If you could do anything in the world and not fail at it, what would you do?"

Pointless question, Jack thought. Real people can't just do whatever they want.

Several people shot back responses that were at least half-serious. "Play professional golf." "Gamble for a living." "Take over the company." "Retire at thirty-five."

Jack had heard them all before. Over the past decade he must have sat through half a dozen seminars like this one. They were supposed to help you better understand yourself and make your work and your whole life more effective and gratifying. Jack didn't mind learning more about himself, but he despised being put in a box and labeled for who he was supposed to be or how he was certain to act in various circumstances. At the last seminar, they said he was a beaver—something about being creative and a hard worker. At the one before that, they pegged him as melancholic, which infuriated him. True, he wasn't exactly the life of every party, but he did have a few friends that he could have a good time with just about anywhere.

He should have looked forward to getting out of the office for these things, but they always got under his skin. Plus he hated sitting still for hours.

His mind was drifting.

Become an artist. That's what I'd do.

When he was a boy, Jack's hobby had been art. He would draw on anything he could find: scrap paper, gum wrappers, pizza boxes—anything. He could sketch a fairly realistic face when he was only five. For years his mom kept the refrigerator covered first with his finger paintings, then with his colored-pencil drawings, and then with his watercolors.

But he hadn't picked up a brush since his twelfth birthday.

Jack scribbled on the fake twenty with his superfine-point pen, shadowing Andrew Jackson's face and profile until his identity began to change. He flipped the bill over and added lines around a couple of the White House windows, growing them into doors. He added a tiny handle and hinges to each one as his mind backtracked.

Heaven? Do you know for sure? If you died today?

He crumpled the paper and pushed it back in his pocket. 11:59.

The seminar leader clicked on a slide showing a Far Side cartoon with a herd of cows at a museum. Chuckles sounded throughout the room. Jack didn't think it was funny. Something about it made him recall his father. He pushed the thought away.

Overhead, the fluorescent lights flickered on. "We'll see you back in an hour," the leader called out as everyone stood.

"Hey, Jack!" The shout came from the back of the room where some of his department coworkers were sitting. "Wanna join us for Chinese?"

Jack turned as he stretched his shoulders and arms. "No thanks, Greg. I have to take care of some stuff." It wasn't totally a lie. He just didn't feel like being with these guys, none of whom he counted among his real friends.

Real friends. At this time in his life, Jack counted four of them for sure—an assessment he'd made just last week while taking stock of his life on his birthday, when he turned thirty-four.

Jack further stretched his stiff muscles as the room quickly emptied, leaving him standing alone in the place he'd been so desperate to escape only moments earlier. He cracked his neck by slowly moving his head back and forth a few times. It was a bad habit, but he'd done it ever since he'd fallen backward while roller-skating in his junior high years. It happened at his fourteenth birthday party during his first couple's skate—it was with Sydney.

Holding on to the memory, Jack put on his navy blue suit jacket, which had been draped on the back of his chair, then stepped out of the conference room and down the empty hallway toward the hotel lobby.

He'd never forgotten that look of concern on Sydney's face after he'd fallen. At the time, as he lay there trying to get back his breath, the pain was more than worth it.

Twenty years ago. Where had the time gone?

Then he replayed the angry conversation they'd had just last night, the kind of conversation that had become so common for him and Sydney. *Where had they gone wrong?* The question brought a twisting ache in his stomach. But the papers would be signed in a few weeks, and it would all be over.

A fresh start, he thought as he pushed the lobby doors open and stepped outside.

12:09.

Just being outdoors made him feel better. The sun was bright, and he covered his eyes with a pair of horn-rimmed sunglasses as he headed down the street, his dress shoes clicking as he walked. Sunlit posters in a travel agency window briefly brought to mind strolls on Caribbean beaches with Sydney on their St. Bart's honeymoon. Those moments now seemed too far away to have ever been real.

At the corner, he stopped to push the crosswalk button. As he waited, his eyes flicked upward to a massive billboard atop a brick building across the street. With white block letters on a black background, it looked like a movie ad:

Feel the agony.

Experience the pain.

Witness the triumph.

Don't miss...THE THORN.

Reading more, he saw it wasn't a movie, but some kind of church production. In the dark background was the grim figure of a man's head, Jesus with a crown of thorns. Blood dripped down his cheeks and from his chin.

Jack knew the story. He'd seen the Mel Gibson *Passion* movie with Sydney, and for days afterward they actually stopped bickering. It was weird the way the film's images stayed with them. Sydney told him she couldn't understand why Jesus seemed so determined to die. She couldn't get over it. Jack had wondered, too, why Jesus didn't simply take a stand for truth and fight back.

The traffic light changed. Jack took another glance upward at the billboard as he crossed the street. Then a surge of music broke into his thoughts.

He loosened his tie as he walked and began mouthing the words to Simon and Garfunkel's "Mrs. Robinson" blaring over loudspeakers above a café's sidewalk tables.

And here's to you, Mrs. Robinson…

Nearing the next corner, he was tempted to enter an art gallery but kept walking. The street scene itself was like an art display to him—looking down the block, he took in the entire perspective, noting the interplay of shapes and angles from the storefronts and shop windows and mentally accenting their colors as if he were conceiving a portrait of the place.

The music kept trailing him.

Jesus loves you more than you could know. Wo, wo, wo…

The aroma here was a mixture of carnival food and exhaust. Just in front of him was a vendor selling hot dogs and sodas. Popcorn and cotton candy, too, just like at the circus. The smells made Jack remember a day when he'd left work early so he and Sydney could take the kids to a traveling fair. Sydney bent over laughing when they discovered little Judd trying to stuff as much pink cotton candy as possible into the mouth of one of the twins in their double stroller. Jack had since forgotten whether it was Andy or Maggie. For some reason the whole thing had struck Sydney as hilarious. Her hysterics got Jack to laughing uncontrollably as the kids stared at them wide-eyed.

The twins would have been barely a year old at the time and Judd five. Almost four years had gone by since then. The pink cotton-candy day—it was a good one. *I need more of those*, Jack thought.

He'd considered buying a hot dog from the vendor but now decided he really wasn't hungry after all and kept walking. He turned a corner and came to an open, brick-paved plaza. He stopped and joined the crowd listening to a one-man band, a leathery old man sitting on a foldout camp stool and holding an accordion. A string connected his left foot to some cymbals, and a horn and harmonica protruded from over the accordion's backside. Out of the apparent chaos of his getup, the man played an old gospel number with all the style and soul of the best band out of New Orleans.

He wore sunglasses, and a white walking cane lay next to his feet on the bricks. For just a brief moment, Jack wondered for some reason if the guy might be faking blindness.

When the song ended, the crowd eagerly applauded. A few onlookers tossed bills into a flipped-over straw hat at the man's feet, the kind of hat they used to punch fists through in old movies.

Jack made his way forward. He leaned over the man and added twenty dollars to the hat, making sure he didn't throw in the fake bill.

The man lifted his head slightly, apparently sensing Jack's presence. "Thank you, Jack," he said hoarsely.

Jack froze. *How does he know my name?*

The raspy voice continued. "And are you ready?"

Jack whispered a reply. "What do you…? But how did you…?"

"I said, 'Are you ready?'"

"Uh—yeah. I guess. But…"

Suddenly aware of the staring crowd, Jack stood and shrugged, then moved along down the sidewalk. When he heard a few notes sounding again from the accordion, he glanced over his shoulder. The musician's head was turned toward Jack, staring at him with blind eyes. Looking right through him.

Jack turned and walked faster, sensing eyes on his back.

Ready? For what? He quickly crossed another street and checked his watch.

12:27.

Last Words

III≡

Still pondering the music man's question, Jack came to the next stoplight and waited as cars sped by. Growing impatient, he stepped off the curb when he saw a break in the traffic.

Then came a sudden flash of red, about chest high. A red Mini Cooper peeled by him, missing him by no more than a foot. The driver stuck his hand out the open window and yelled something unintelligible.

Jack's heart raced as he stepped back onto the sidewalk, where a handful of people still waited for the walk signal. "People need to watch where they're going," he said aloud, meaning the driver.

He cracked his neck again and hoped the worst of his day was over.

In the next block, he passed a Starbucks with an open-air patio tucked in front of it. Remembering how bad the coffee was at the seminar, he decided a vanilla latte was what he needed to survive the afternoon.

As Jack stepped inside and joined the line behind a very large woman, his cell phone rang. He pulled it from his jacket pocket and looked at his caller ID. It was Sydney—the LCD read "SUGAR," and he reminded himself again for the umpteenth time to reprogram that label. Somehow he'd never got around to doing it.

"Hey," he answered curtly. The lady in line turned and looked at him in surprise. Jack smiled and motioned to his cell phone.

"Jack, we've got some trouble," Sydney said in her latest get-to-the-point manner. "Judd's teacher called and said he's been in a fight. Something about throwing pine cones at one of the girls. I thought you were going to talk to him about that stuff, Jack."

It never took her long anymore to launch into him. "It's okay, Syd. I'll take care of it."

"That's what you said last time. I thought you were going to meet with the principal last week, and you said you'd talk to Judd." Sydney was talking faster, which always made Jack nervous.

He forced himself to speak calmly. "Please, Sydney, not now. I promise I'll take care of it. Don't worry."

He covered the phone's mike and ordered his coffee.

"How are the twins?" he asked in a level tone.

"Fine," she said tersely. "Maggie marked all over herself with my lipsticks. And Andy's been sulking all morning. I heard him saying 'Nobody loves me' to his teddy bear."

Give me a break, Jack thought. "So let me guess—now you'd like me to have a talk with Andy about lying to his teddy bear?"

"It's not funny, Jack," Sydney snapped. The kids had been the only reason they could find to stay together, but finally even that wasn't enough.

Her voice softened a bit. "Anyway, Maggie came to his rescue. She's making him play house with her."

"Serves him right," Jack said.

"How's the seminar?" she asked, without a hint of real interest.

"Great," Jack said as sarcastically as he could. "Learning lots. Terrific stuff. We can only hope the world's really ready for such a new and improved me."

"Right." She wasn't buying it.

There was a pause. "Jack." Her voice was even softer. "Jack, I…there's one thing, one more thing that I…"

"Yeah?"

The reception was breaking up. He listened for a comeback, then checked the signal strength. He'd lost her. With a shrug, he dropped the phone back in his coat pocket.

He crossed his arms and stared out the coffee shop window. *Where had things gone wrong?* It used to be so different between them, so alive. Maybe it was just the work and having kids and not being young anymore.

Send her flowers, he told himself, surprising himself with the thought. But no, not now. That was too personal, the wrong signal.

The guy behind the counter set a latte on the counter and called his name.

The place was filling up with the after-lunch crowd. Jack picked up his coffee and made his way to the patio outside. Just beyond the doorway, an old woman in a wheelchair was blocking his way. She was sitting there with her back to him, whistling a tune. Jack waited impatiently for a few moments before pushing around her. Knocking against her chair handle as he passed, he noticed a bulky quilt hiding her legs.

"Oh, please excuse me, sir," the woman said, "and I hope you have a wonderful day." Jack didn't look back.

The outdoor patio took up one corner of the establishment. It was bordered by the windowless brick wall of the old two-story building next door, which quickly caught Jack's eye. He thought the well-aged, roughly laid bricks formed the perfect backdrop for this outdoor café. He found a table near the ancient wall and sat down. Bob Dylan's "Hey, Mr. Tambourine Man" played over the sound system. Thrumming his fingers on the table, Jack glanced around.

In the jingle jangle morning I'll come followin' you.

Jack was a people watcher. At one table he saw a guy with a small pair of headphones shoved in his ears clicking away on an Apple PowerBook. Jack placed him in his twenties. He was bushy-haired, with a beard to match, and was wearing thick-framed glasses, worn-out khaki shorts, and a T-shirt that said *Bowl at Ed's* in big letters. He tapped his scraggly flip-flops to the music as he worked. He smiled and occasionally sang out a few soft words as he tapped away at the keyboard. Jack watched his lips as he tossed his head and sang out, *"Call me the underdog…"*

Jack imagined the guy to be a freelance graphic artist. No wife, no boss, hardly a care in the world. *What a life.* It was the life Jack wanted. No suits, no expense reports, no company seminars. Freedom.

He sighed at the thought. So often in the past few years he'd contemplated going to work for himself. *Someday*, he mused as he studied Underdog's face. *Someday soon.*

Not far from the flip-flop dude, the woman in the wheelchair had pulled up and parked herself. Pulling a newspaper out of her frumpy handbag, she busied herself with a crossword puzzle. *Why was she smiling?* For some reason the old woman irritated Jack. He imagined her always expecting special treatment and not even trying to walk on her own. *Hey, we've all got our share of problems*, he thought.

Jack turned away from her and took another sip of his coffee.

"Why, Alexis, you haven't changed at all," a raised voice said at the table next to him. It belonged to an older man with salt-and-pepper hair and goatee wearing a flannel shirt, fleece vest, and a floppy fishing hat. Facing him was a young attractive woman dressed to the nines. Jack couldn't help overhearing their conversation. Eavesdropping came easy to a people watcher.

The man spoke with a faint British accent that vaguely reminded Jack of Alistair Cooke. "You're as passionate about justice as you've always been," he continued, pausing every few words for effect. "Once, it was in my classroom. Now, it's in the courtroom."

The woman lightly tapped a thumbnail against her lower lip. Jack couldn't help noticing her stunning facial features and her blond hair shining in the sunlight. The smoothness of her voice was a perfect match for her looks. "You're right, Professor," she said. "But true passion for justice can drive an attorney crazy. Or anyway, I think that's what this case is doing to me. Look, a *little girl* was this man's victim, yet it appears he'll get off scot-free."

She raised her chin and shook her head in frustration, her hair dancing in the light. Then she leaned in closer. "So I need your help. There's obviously no chance for a conviction if this pile of so-called insanity evidence keeps building. My job is simple: Prove he's not crazy—prove he knew exactly what he was doing. And you could see through any insanity bull better than anyone I know—and help others see through it, too. 'We're all responsible for our actions'—that's always been the hallmark of your philosophical viewpoint. If I heard you say it in class once, I heard it a thousand times." Her voice was strong and clear. Jack liked her.

"But you know I'm no criminal expert," the man answered. "I'm just a philosophy nut, remember?" He winked as he rotated the brown sleeve wrapped around his coffee cup. "I want to help you, Alexis, I sincerely do. But from everything you've explained so far, I'd say it's very reasonable to conclude that if this guy isn't already over the edge, he's as close as he can get. Are you *totally* sure he's faking it?"

She dropped her shoulders. "No, not totally. But I've got to do whatever I can to help this girl. *That's* what I'm sure of."

He nodded.

She smiled at him. "So…can you help me?"

The older man smiled back but made no commitment.

Dylan was still crooning in the background. *Hey, Mr. Tambourine Man, play a song for me. I'm not sleepy and there is no place I'm goin' to….*

Jack sipped his coffee again and glanced at his watch. 12:46. Soon he would need to start walking back to the seminar. He had just turned his head to glance across the patio when someone screamed from the street.

"Look out!" someone on the patio yelled.

Jack didn't need to be told where to look. A huge truck was careening across the sidewalk, angled straight for the patio's outer corner. As the roar of the truck's engine intensified, so did the shouts and screams from every side. Unable to take his eyes off the truck, Jack had only enough time to jump to his feet and stumble back a step. An instant later, he heard the thunderous crash and crumpling of metal as the truck slammed dead center into the corner of the brick wall next to the patio, sending a visible tremor through the entire structure.

As the demolished truck came to a halt, Jack thought for a split second that the nightmare was over. But a movement caught his eye, and he jerked his head upward.

The brick wall was collapsing.

As if in slow motion, the falling wall of bricks began to block out the sky above him as a new wave of screams erupted all around. Instinctively he turned to run, but it was too late. He felt his back and head being pounded.

The next thing he knew, he was no longer running, no longer even on his feet. The back of his head throbbed with pain. He tried to reach up to it, but he couldn't move. He tried calling for help, but his throat kept choking with dust.

He opened his eyes—or at least he thought he did—but there was only darkness. He heard himself moan.

Stay awake, he told himself. *Come on, fight this thing.*

It was no use. Jack felt himself drifting, his mind spinning.

He was going.

He was gone.

Floating

||| ≡

Jack thought he was fainting. Then sliding—downward, forward, backward, in all directions. Yet his hands and arms and legs felt tight and closed, his chest compressed, his body confined. A sort of pressure filled his brain and made him light and foggy and unable to connect his thoughts. Everything was muted, slow, dark.

The pressure in his head intensified, as if he were pushing himself up through his own skull. It happened slowly, yet all at once.

Then another sensation: He was rising, lifting like a kite catching a breeze. Quick flashes of light swept over his eyelids.

His eyes blinked open. Air filled his lungs as he gasped for breath.

What happened?

He seemed to have some kind of tunnel vision that blurred his peripheral sight. As he looked around, his gaze was quickly drawn downward, and his mind struggled to register what his eyes were seeing.

Jack wasn't on the coffee shop patio anymore. Somehow, he was above it. Or rather, looking down on what was left of it. Everywhere the air was full of dust, but through the haze he quickly recognized the coffee shop. The dust hung heaviest over the place where the little outdoor patio had been, now mostly covered in jagged heaps of bricks and debris. Jutting out from the wreckage, straddling the sidewalk, was the massive rear portion of the truck.

He stared at it all with a strange calmness, as if what he was seeing no longer had any real link to him.

Where am I? How did I get thrown up here? A thought came to mind that he should be afraid of falling. It was at least a twenty-foot drop to the ground. But that notion in his brain didn't connect at all with his body. Something— some eerie tranquility—was overriding any fear.

The dust cleared some, and he saw movement below— people rushing on the sidewalk and in the street. He looked closer and could see their mouths moving. They were talking, but he couldn't hear them. Why was everything so silent?

In the same second these thoughts came to him, he began hearing the voices below, as if he'd just pressed the volume button on a TV remote. He detected shouts and screams, but the sounds were garbled or muffled, as if a huge invisible blanket had been thrown over everything.

Something must have happened to his hearing. Jack reached up and rubbed his fingers on his temples as he continued staring below, unable to break his gaze.

At the rubble's edge, a few people were being pulled from the debris, helped out by the gathering crowd. The victims were bleeding badly. Other people nearby were crying and embracing.

Here and there on the ground, large sections of the fallen wall were still together in jagged, ugly pieces where they'd landed, but the collapse of the wall had turned a good portion of it into countless loose bricks and shards of mortar. A few guys were already pulling away some of the dusty wreckage piece by piece, digging for victims. Jack saw a man in an apron—the man from behind the counter who'd mixed his latte—pulling bricks from a place where the twisted frames of some of the metal tables and chairs were sticking out at the edges of the rubble.

A couple of uniformed police, a man and a woman, came running up and began taking charge, moving most of the people back, then assisting the ones who were searching in the bricks.

Jack's vision zeroed in on the spot where the guy in the apron was working. His sight was focused on the man's quickly moving hands—already ash white from the mortar dust. In a moment, he turned and yelled something at the policeman, who quickly came to his side and joined in the work.

Someone was buried there. Jack saw some dark clothing, then the heel of a man's dress shoe. The two rescuers were working upward to the person's torso and head, not bothering yet to fully uncover the legs.

A siren wailed, and Jack saw flashing emergency lights, but he couldn't turn his sight from the two men working frantically below.

They uncovered the person's head. It was facedown and red with blood, the hair showing dark underneath all the dust. The policeman reached in and placed his hand on the person's throat, feeling for a pulse.

More sirens screamed, and the entire area surged with action and movement. But Jack kept his eyes locked on the single rescue he'd been following.

Finally, the awkwardly sprawled figure was fully uncovered. It was a man in a dark suit. Other people in uniforms hurried over and crowded around him, blocking Jack's view. They carefully turned over the guy's limp form, then carried it beyond the rubble to a clear spot on the sidewalk. As the rescuers stepped back and opened up his view again, Jack squinted, and somehow that action seemed to zoom his vision down closer.

He found himself staring into a lifeless, pale-gray face.

His own face.

Jack held his breath. His mind seemed fogged in again, and all the sounds from below began fading away as he kept his eyes on that face. *His* face.

Everything from the past several minutes came back to him in a wave. His logical mind lined it up, rehearsing it all as if to confirm what he was seeing with his own eyes. He'd walked into Starbucks. There was the cut-off phone call from Sydney and the vanilla latte. He'd sat down at a table outside, right by the brick wall. He'd watched Underdog with the computer. Heard the blond lady pleading with her professor friend.

He'd just looked out to the street when someone yelled, and there was that crazy truck hurtling right at them. People screamed, and the truck kept coming until it crashed into the wall there at the corner of the building. Then that huge wall seemed to collapse in upon itself, and down it came. He ran. The bricks smashed into his shoulders and head. Then nothing.

I died. I must have died.

Jack raised a hand and felt the back of his head. He felt no pain. His eyes blinked tears, but he didn't know why. He found himself taking short, sudden breaths.

The scene below began to fade, and the sounds died away. He strained his eyes to see himself on that sidewalk, but the picture slipped away like water into a storm drain.

And then there was nothing. Nothing at all.

The sky around him didn't seem real; it was more like the blue screen on a movie set, only it was moving. There were no clouds or birds, and the whole thing seemed to spin and swirl, like a giant, slowly turning spiral.

He took a step back, then another, yet there was nothing to step on. He was neither falling nor standing, but floating.

He shook his head. In exasperation, he called aloud, "What's happening?"

"Yeah!" someone said. "That's what I want to know."

The voice came from above him.

Jack looked up. Ten feet beyond and above him, he saw a man standing in the air, unattached to anything, with his hands on his hips. It was bushy-haired Underdog, and he stared at Jack with his eyes and mouth wide open. He still had on the khaki shorts and the T-shirt and the flip-flops.

That's when Jack looked down and realized he was still wearing his suit—or at least some ghostly version of it. He clasped his wrist, clutching the navy-blue sleeve. *Great*, he thought, *dressed for business even here*.

It seemed so crazy, so wild. *It's only a dream*. He shut his eyes tight.

"Hey, man…" It was Underdog's voice again. "Are you…are you, like, an angel?"

Jack looked up again. Confused as he was, he couldn't keep from grinning. "Nobody ever called me *that* before."

"But—you're here to take me to heaven, aren't you?" The guy looked and sounded sincere.

The moment Jack decided to move closer, he found himself standing next to the flip-flop guy, as if the thought itself had silently moved him there. "Listen," Jack said, "I think I'm in the same boat you are. I mean…I was down there, too. Where the wall fell." He pointed to where he had been on the patio. "Only a minute ago, I think. And before it happened, I remember seeing you—with your computer."

Underdog nodded. "So…this is it for both of us?"

"Uhh…yeah, whatever 'it' is."

Underdog's face lit up with a wide toothy smile. "*Awesome!*" He drew as near as possible to Jack and thrust out his hand. "I'm Elliott!"

Jack shook his hand. It felt solid, like a real hand.

"I'm Jack."

"*Jack!* So we're in it together. Right, Jack?" Elliott was still pumping his arm.

"Uhh…so it appears."

"*Awesome! Yes!*" Elliott finally let go of his hand.

Jack instantly liked Elliott. He reminded him of one of his high school friends, Ricky McLindy. The day after graduation, the two of them had jumped into Jack's '67 Volkswagen bus and taken a three-month tour out west. Along the way, they talked about everything—their backgrounds, their plans and dreams, the women they loved. It was on that trip that Jack decided to marry Sydney.

Elliott smiled from ear to ear as he restlessly turned around, peering in every direction. "So what happens next?" he asked. "Do we wait here? Or should we, like, try floating on up? Or what exactly?"

Jack felt a surge of pleasure in hearing Elliott seek his guidance, even if he had none to offer at the moment. Jack again scanned the strange blueness all around them. But before he could say anything, he saw Elliott pump his fists in the air and erupt with a shout.

"*Wo!* I can hardly believe this! It's just absolutely incredible! Do you know it was only last week I got everything squared away with him? Man, Jack, this is just totally, incredibly amazing!"

Jack smiled at his new friend's joy, but the words puzzled him. Elliott must have taken out some huge life insurance policy a week ago. If so, the insurance agent clearly was not going to be as ecstatic about it today as Elliott was. Somehow, though, Jack couldn't quite imagine this young guy having a wife and kids to leave anything to. So what would make him so happy?

Elliott clasped his fists in front of him and turned to Jack. "Isn't this *exciting?*"

"I...I hope it will be, Elliott." He tried to sound wise. "But I think we're just going to have to wait and see, and—you know—try to get a grip on what we're really facing here."

Elliott laughed and slapped Jack on the back in a playful way. "Well, whatever it is, it's for sure gonna be *good!* It's gonna be one wild ride, Jack buddy." He slapped his hands together. "Bring...it...ON!"

This guy seemed so utterly and unfoundedly confident. Jack wondered where the personality seminars would peg somebody like this. *Crazy*, maybe. "I like your attitude, Elliott," he told him, forcing a smile. "I really do."

With a jerk, Elliott turned his bushy head toward Jack. "I got it! Let's call out to him. Yeah! I feel like yelling."

"What do you mean? Call out to who?"

Elliott spread his feet, dropped back his head, stared upward, and bellowed with ear-splitting volume, *"GODDDD!"*

God, Jack thought. *God, what is this?* His experience here was beginning to give him the creeps.

Just then, a woman's voice came echoing out of the blue. "God! O God, *no!*"

In the air only twenty feet beyond them, a woman suddenly materialized with a man standing next to her. It was the blond attorney from the coffee shop, plus the professor, still wearing his absurd floppy hat.

Despite Elliott's wild scream, they seemed totally unaware that anyone else was there. They both were staring intensely at something below them. The professor clasped her hands in his while she shook her head in disbelief. "It can't be. It just can't be!"

Elliott began moving toward them, then paused. Jack followed, becoming more accustomed to moving on air. He stood at Elliott's side.

"That's us," the professor whispered, his vision locked downward. "See? Those are our bodies they're moving."

"No. *No,* don't tell me that," the woman answered. She turned her head and closed her eyes. "This is a dream, some nightmare."

"Please be calm, Alexis. No, this is no dream. It's no

hallucination or anything. This is real. I'm quite sure it's the real thing." He let go of her hand.

She took a step away from him. "The real *what*? What do you mean? Sure of *what*? Don't say those things! We can't be sure, and you know it!"

"Calm down, Alexis, please."

"Hey!" Elliott shouted as he bounded toward them, unable to wait any longer.

Startled, they both jumped.

Jack drew closer to them as well.

The woman's eyes flared. The sight of the two unexpected companions seemed to trigger a new mood in her, a steely calmness. Alexis stepped forward, her chin raised and her back stiff.

"Who are you?" she asked like a cross-examining lawyer.

"I'm Elliott!" He kept smiling. "And my buddy here is Jack."

"All right. I want to know what's going on here. Is this some kind of joke?"

"Not really, but it's still okay to laugh," Elliott answered. "Lighten up!"

"I don't have time for this," Alexis snapped. "Just tell me: Were you down there?" She pointed below.

"You bet I was," Elliott answered. "And so was Jack."

"Then I want you to tell me exactly what happened."

Standing behind her, the professor sighed. "Alexis, we're already quite aware of what happened. You know, and I know."

She closed her eyes and shook her head before shrugging off his words. She glared again at Elliott, who grinned as if this were some kind of game.

"Tell me," she demanded. "Did you see the driver of that truck?"

The professor put his hand on her shoulder. "Alexis, my dear—"

"Did you?"

"Alexis," the professor interrupted again, "it doesn't matter anymore."

"*Did you?*" she asked Elliott once more. Then she turned to Jack. "I want answers *now*."

Jack saw the professor's fingers tighten on her shoulder. "You must stop this, Alexis," he told her more firmly.

Her shoulders drooped, the tenseness drained from her face, and she looked ready to burst into tears. "Whatever this is," she said, "wherever we are, I know my life can't be over." The hardness was gone from her voice, replaced by desperation. "It *cannot* be over." She looked in turn into all their faces, pleading. "This can't be the end. Just tell me that much, please!"

"Oh, lighten up, for heaven's sake," Elliott said, his smile blazing strong as ever. "Of course this isn't the end. You're standing there, aren't you?"

At that moment, another voice echoed out of the blue, another woman's voice, this time singing,

And I see you standing there!
Oh yes, I see you standing there!

Just as quickly, the voice's owner appeared nearby. It belonged to a slender elderly woman with white hair, chocolate-brown arms stretched wide in greeting, and a smile even brighter than the lemon-yellow flower-print dress she was wearing.

"I do, I do!" she said with a laugh. "I *do* see you all standing there! And don't you see me, too?" She spun around for them, her arms still outstretched. She seemed giddy, almost drunk.

Looking closer, Jack abruptly realized this was the woman in the wheelchair on the coffee shop patio. But the wheelchair was nowhere in sight, and she was walking—or rather, dancing—her way toward them.

"My name's Millie," she continued. "And I'm so *glad* to see you all, and so glad to *be* with you all, right here in the ever-after!"

This was too much for Alexis, who definitely looked as if she'd seen a ghost. "This is crazy! You're all crazy," she sobbed. "We aren't dead, and there is no—whatever-after."

A crease of compassion appeared on Millie's forehead. She looked at Alexis with an expression that at once suggested a deep love and a deeper secret. "Oh, child," she said as she held out her hand.

Alexis drew back in defiance. "For crying out loud, I'm not a child. I'm an adult with a rational mind, and there *is* a way, somehow, to get a coherent, satisfying explanation for all this. Somebody somewhere can tell me the truth." She looked ready to bolt. To run somewhere, anywhere.

Once more, a voice startled them by coming from nowhere.

"*Here's* the truth," the voice declared in a gruff tone, suggesting at once that the truth might not be something Jack particularly wanted to hear.

A Journey Begins

∥≡

The figure that materialized before them had the look of a workingman. He had sun-worn skin, a deeply lined face that looked accustomed to scowling, and dark hair that was tangled and tousled. It would be easy to assume he was just another fresh accident victim from below, except that the accident would have to have been at a bar instead of a Starbucks.

His attire, however, set him distinctly apart from the others in this little group. He wore some kind of sleeveless robe made of coarse, grayish-brown cloth that fell loosely from his broad shoulders to his well-defined calves. He was barefoot, except for what looked like faded strips of rags wrapped narrowly around the arches of both feet. The same kind of narrow strips were bound around his wrists, slightly overlapping the base of both hands.

All in all, Jack doubted this guy's style would ever catch on.

Alexis wrinkled her face. "Who are you?" she demanded.

The workingman stepped closer, stood in front of them, and squinted for a moment, as if looking into the sun. Jack thought of the Marlboro Man in the old cigarette ads.

Unexpectedly, the new arrival broke into a smile. "I'm Nate," he said with more warmth in his voice, though not enough to conceal his apparent natural gruffness.

He was looking them over. "Hello, Jack," he said. "Good to see you."

"How do you know my name?" Jack asked. *Is this guy some kind of angel?* His mind raced back to his experience with the old music man playing on the street corner.

Nate's face brightened with a bigger smile. He pointed silently to Jack's chest.

Reaching up, Jack felt the peel-and-stick name tag that was still on his coat lapel from the seminar, with its preprinted greeting: HELLO, my name is JACK GATES. Jack peeled it off and crumpled it into his pocket, grinning sheepishly back at Nate.

He noticed the trace of a scar running below Nate's ear. Then a thought struck him.

"Wait a minute." He jabbed a finger in Nate's direction. "I bet I know who you are. You're the truck driver, aren't you? The guy who crashed into that wall."

Alexis gave out a quick little gasp.

"You're wrong," Nate quickly replied. "I'm not that man."

Jack wasn't so sure. "Then where is he?"

"He hasn't died yet."

"But the front of that truck was demolished," Jack argued. "That driver had to get hammered."

"He hasn't died yet."

"But…how can you be so sure?"

"Do you see him here?"

"Well…no."

"He hasn't died yet." Nate was unflinching.

Alexis had had enough of these rabbit trails. She took a bold step forward to interrogate Nate. "You said you've got the truth," she said. "So what do you have to tell us? Where are we?"

Elliott was just as impatient, but without being bugged. "We're in heaven, right?" He nodded energetically.

Nate took a step toward them, then stood silently for a moment with a no-nonsense expression that sent a slight chill up Jack's neck. The guy couldn't escape looking like a loser, but somehow he managed to command definite authority over them. *Maybe*, Jack thought, *it's only because the rest of us are still so filled with uncertainty about our new surroundings.*

Nate spoke up, still in his husky tone. "I'm taking you to the Two Doors. Each of you will enter only one of them, by a choice that's out of my hands. Now, follow me."

He turned and began walking into the nothingness with hefty strides.

"That's all?" Alexis was incredulous. She looked around at the group as Nate continued walking away. "What kind of explanation is *that*?"

Millie apparently needed no clarification, and she eagerly stepped out to follow Nate. So did Elliott.

Holding back, Jack exchanged glances with Alexis and the professor. "You know," Jack whispered, "I'm not sure I trust our self-appointed tour guide. Something about him seems out of place."

The professor nodded. "But then, everything's out of place here," he said. "Actually, I don't think we have much choice at the moment except to follow him."

"That's insane," Alexis retorted.

"Perhaps," said the professor, "but so is just standing here waiting."

"But this could be some kind of trick," Alexis said. "That guy has criminal written all over him."

"Come on, Alexis," the professor said, "what more have we got to lose?" He quickly stepped forward to follow Nate, not waiting for Alexis and Jack to decide.

Alexis stared at Jack. Fear flashed in her eyes, revealing a cold panic that surprised and unnerved him. As beautiful as she was, Jack realized he would hate to be stuck here alone with her.

She must have come to the same conclusion about Jack. She turned and hurried to catch up with the others.

Jack hesitated only a moment, then followed, a cold dread growing heavier in his mind.

Despite Nate's rapid pace, it wasn't hard for the travelers—even old Millie—to keep up with him. There was a definite sense of exertion in the walk, but Jack never felt any shortness of breath or tiredness.

Jack couldn't fathom how Nate knew where they were or what direction they were headed, because the scene around them was so disorienting. It was obvious they were in some huge expanse, but it had no horizon to give them any bearings. The vastness seemed to stretch just as far below as it did above and around them.

Even so, they seemed to be making some kind of progress. As they walked along, the appearance of their surroundings revealed subtle shifts in color, texture, and even mood.

At first, the stark blueness continued to intensify, looking crisper than any fair sky Jack had ever viewed from earth. This eventually transformed into a misty gray, almost as if they'd unknowingly entered a massive cumulus cloud. In time, they came to stretches where traces of rich green and warm yellow and even glints of red seemed to dance in the air, as if colored curtains of some impossibly thin gauze were suspended around them just out of reach.

Jack felt both fascination and lingering fear. Looking at the others, he couldn't tell if they felt the same mix of emotions. They walked beside one another in silence, keeping their thoughts to themselves.

True to old habits, Jack glanced at his watch.

The display read 12:46.

He stared at the numbers, unable to comprehend what they could mean. *Impossible*, he thought.

He tried to calculate how much time had passed since…since this all began. He must have spent at least ten to twelve minutes watching the rescuers uncover his body from the rubble. Then maybe five minutes talking with Elliott, followed by another ten to twelve as the others appeared in view, then another three to five after Nate showed up. A minimum of a good half hour right there. And now they'd been walking for…what? Twenty minutes? Thirty?

Of course, time often seems to pass more slowly when you're in new situations. At any rate, Jack figured they must have been walking for at least twelve to fifteen minutes.

He stared at his watch once more. 12:46. Jack was sure it had to be 1:30 in the afternoon at the absolute earliest, and more likely closer to two o'clock.

But then…what difference does that make now?

In the same moment, he detected a sudden dimming of the light around them. It was as if the curtains he'd imagined hanging there were becoming grayer, thicker, darker. He felt the impulse to catch up to Nate and talk to him.

Their guide had been staying consistently about three strides in front of the group. Jack picked up his pace to cover the distance, but he couldn't get closer. Nate didn't appear to be going any faster; Jack simply couldn't overtake him. So he fell back again with the others.

Stepping again beside Alexis and the professor, he looked at each of them, and in silent agreement, the three pulled back a few steps behind Elliott and Millie, who were talking quietly with each other.

"What is this accomplishing?" Alexis murmured under her breath. "I still need more information."

"I doubt we'll be getting any," Jack whispered. "Not on our timetable, anyway. This whole thing seems to grow more obscure by the moment."

"Precisely," she said. "This is pointless. I'm going to speak up. I'm going to insist that we stop here and now and talk this thing through and get some answers. We deserve that much, at least. We have a right to know the facts."

"You're probably right," the professor said softly. "Maybe it's best, however, for someone else to do the talking. Let me approach Nate."

Alexis glared at the professor.

Jack ignored her. "Sounds good," he told the professor. "Let him have it, loud and clear."

"And any suggestions on how I should word our request?"

"Get right to the point," Jack counseled him. "Nate doesn't seem to be one for chitchat."

The professor continued. "And the 'point' that I should quickly get to—what is it exactly?"

"Well…I suspect we'll keep hiking along like this until those two doors he mentioned pop up out of nowhere," Jack said. "I figure at least one of them must be an escape from this place, and that's ultimately what we're after, right? Apparently, we get to choose which door we want. But without knowing more particulars, we could easily get stuck with the wrong choice."

"So," the professor agreed, "everything more or less comes down to our getting further details regarding those two doors."

Jack nodded, then looked up with a start when Nate's voice suddenly blared from out front: "The two doors!" The way he said it made Jack sense immediately that their guide had heard every word they'd whispered.

Nate was still pacing forward as he called back to them over his shoulder. "One door is for eternal life; one door is for eternal death."

It was spooky, Jack thought, the way he said it.

"Eternal death—that means hell," Elliott added soberly. Jack chafed at that.

"How do *you* know?" Alexis asked, stealing the question right out of Jack's mouth. She shot her words at Elliott like a cannon. "You mean hell being some actual place, hell as a reality? I don't even believe in hell! That can't be what it is."

"Well, ask him," Elliott replied casually, pointing to their guide. Millie silently nodded.

"All right," the professor interjected. "We will." He raised his chin and looked firmly ahead. "Nate! You seem to be implying there's one doorway opening to heaven and another doorway leading to…to hell, shall we say."

Up ahead, Nate didn't slow down or look back. Meanwhile, the professor's voice began losing punch with every word he spoke. "I…I have to say, Nate, that if this assumption is correct, the manner in which you've expressed these things is confusing and…well, it rather tends to represent the situation in a manner somewhat different from what we've been led to expect."

Nate abruptly stopped and spun around to face them. "What *did* you expect?" His expression wasn't a scowl, but it was no smile either. He looked directly into each of their faces in turn.

Jack found himself speechless. So were the others.

Turning, Nate resumed his steady walking, leaving them all to answer his question for themselves as they followed.

So what did I expect? Jack wondered.

He'd had his share of thoughts about death, for sure. Not all the time, not even with any frequency, but on occasion—at the handful of funerals he'd attended, for example, or sometimes when he heard about a tragic disaster. Since he'd never been very religious, the question of some mysterious future after death never mattered much.

How could it be? How had he managed to spend so little time thinking about death and what comes after? *It matters now,* he told himself.

Memories flickered in his mind. A basement with a concrete floor painted shiny gray, the basement of a church that Jack hadn't thought about in years. When he was a kid, his parents had regularly gone with him and his younger brother to the little church, and Jack remembered especially the frequent potlucks in the basement—where the kitchen was and the smiling old ladies unwrapping their cakes and casseroles and salads.

He remembered one day when he'd run for refuge to that basement. Upstairs, in the sanctuary, he'd just seen his first dead body. It was old Mr. Kilvens—Jack still remembered the man's name.

When Mr. Kilvens died, Jack's parents decided he was old enough to attend the funeral on that cold, snowy day. Jack remembered the open casket placed at the front of the drafty church with the stained glass windows and how people stood and cried over the man's body and even kissed his lifeless face.

Jack decided that afternoon that he was afraid to die. He was afraid of being a cold dead body in a box and of old people kissing his face when there was nothing he could do about it. Jack knew he wasn't supposed to be afraid of this, but he was.

At one point in the funeral, Jack slipped away and went downstairs to the kitchen. He sat in a metal folding chair in a corner by the roaring furnace and cried and cried until one of the old ladies gave him some green marshmallow salad.

A voice interrupted his thoughts. "So, Jack…" It was the professor, walking next to him. "What did you expect?"

Jack shook his head. The truth was, over the years he'd come to the conclusion that at the moment he died, he'd just putter out and turn off, like hitting "shut down" on a computer.

He turned to the professor. "I suppose I figured that

when you die, you simply disappear…you know, back to the dust and all."

The professor pursed his lips. "It appears that won't be the case, doesn't it?"

Alexis joined their conversation. "What about reincarnation? Maybe that door to eternal life is only the door to coming back to earth as someone or something different."

Jack smiled. He could easily see coming back as a basketball star or a billionaire. Or maybe a horse.

"Or even just returning as a ghost," Alexis continued.

As a kid, Jack had imagined old Mr. Kilvens floating about in their basement at home, and for a while he would dash up the stairs after turning off the lights, just in case.

"Or coming back as energy." Alexis was mulling over every possibility. "What could be more eternal than energy?" As she said it, Jack realized that the light around them was continuing to dim as the gray curtains grew thicker.

Nate's resounding voice sliced into their discussion. "Forget those lies!"

"Eternal life," he said, again speaking over his shoulder as he walked, "is never, even for a moment, anything less than this: living with the infinite One who gives unending joy and pleasure in his presence." Nate didn't state this like a theory from a philosopher or a theologian. It came across as something he knew intimately from everyday personal experience.

Jack looked around at his companions as they all kept walking. Alexis looked more irritated than ever. With a slight jerk of her blond head, she motioned him back for more discussion, but Jack pretended not to see. He was tired of her whining.

The professor simply looked dazed, as well as more foolish than ever. Jack wondered why he hadn't pitched his goofy hat a long time ago.

Elliott wore a playful grin on his face. He reminded Jack more and more of a four-year-old child.

Millie's huge brown eyes welled up with tears—sentimental tears, no doubt, over the last words Nate had spoken.

Still gazing at Millie, Jack caught a dazzling sparkle in her tears, and her eyes grew wide with wonder.

Jack looked ahead. Something like a towering wall of crystal had soared into view, shimmering with light. Around them, all along their pathway, the gray curtains were rapidly growing darker and darker in contrast, until the boldly striding form of Nate in front of them appeared as only a silhouette against the gleaming crystal backdrop. Jack turned to look behind them and saw only black nothingness.

They were nearing the crystal wall much faster than seemed possible—almost as if it were rushing out to meet them. It looked something like a giant sheet of falling water backlit by countless thousands of multicolored floodlights, but Jack detected no sound from it. And the water, or whatever it was, was falling *up* as well as down.

"*Awesome!*" Elliott kept shouting, with his arms upraised. Millie began dancing again.

"That looks absolutely nothing like a door," was all the professor had to say.

Whatever it was, it was closing in fast. They would all be going through it.

Farther In
and Higher Up

⚏

As the crystal barrier broke over him, Jack felt at first as though he were pressing against something like a giant piece of cellophane cling-wrap. He kept trying to move forward, desperate to get through. But something blocked him or held him back.

As he pushed, he began seeing moving pictures. First, just a few—a bee alighting on the petals of a lily, an oak tree's branches tossing in a strong wind, a widening smile on the face of an African child. Then there were dozens, hundreds of images. The space in front and around him was like a giant video screen filled with hundreds, then countless thousands of moving scenes from the earth, changing faster and faster.

Sounds came just as the pictures did. Only a few at first—a dog's bark, a melody from a violin, a woman's laughter and the clink of glasses, a rumble of distant thunder. Then a reverberating onrush of noises and conversations and shouts and songs, until it became an earsplitting roar, like a thousand Niagaras.

The light of the images became so bright that it finally blinded him, and there was only darkness. Everything went black as Jack kept pushing. He kept trying to ram his body forward until he was sure he could push no harder.

Finally, as if breaking the surface of a pool after being submerged from a deep dive, he burst through.

Then the noise ended, the darkness dropped away, and a warm golden light washed over everything. Jack caught his breath at the sight before him.

"It's so *beautiful!*" he heard Millie exclaim. And it was.

Their path now was a curved lane paved with creamy granite stones traversing a rolling meadow of grasses and tiny wildflowers. Clumps of wild rosebushes bloomed brightly near the path.

It was a little island, with the blue sea all around and white seagulls circling and calling as gentle waves sounded on the shores. And songbirds. Some chirped from the rosebushes, while others darted and looped overhead. Everything was bathed in golden light, though no sun appeared in the sky.

A breeze touched his face, and Jack inhaled deeply. The distinct fresh smell of the sea mingled with the fragrance of the roses. He closed his eyes for a moment and inhaled even deeper, listening again to the waves and the gulls and the trilling of the birds.

Nate was still pressing forward in front of them, and Jack and the others still walked along behind as if the shining barrier had never interrupted their journey, as if they'd been on this same smooth lane the whole time. Yet compared to the previous stretch of their journey, this was an entirely different world. The reality of it—the bright, sweet, tangible, touchable firmness of it—was overwhelming.

He heard Elliott laughing as he bent down and swooped his fingers through the waving grass. Jack did it, too.

Nate turned and began walking backward so he could face the group and talk as they continued onward. His strange new smile seemed to indicate that he knew a great, deep, wonderful secret.

"All this," he said, spreading his arms—"God created it all for you, to begin welcoming you into his presence. And you haven't begun to see the best of it!"

Millie looked upward, a broad smile erupting on her face.

Into his presence. Jack couldn't fathom what that could mean. God's presence. *God!* What could he be like? Jack wanted to imagine it, but another part of him resisted the thought.

"I'll be guiding you through the entrance to forever," Nate continued. "There's lots more to tell you, but we've got appointments to keep." He turned back around and began trotting forward. "This way. Let's go!"

They all began running.

They mounted a little rise from where they could see

their pathway curving down to a stone archway above a wood-planked gate. On either side of the gate, the wild grass grew thick in high wavy clumps so they couldn't see what was beyond the arch. A pretty enough setting, but rather understated and low-profile for what Jack had expected next.

Nate stopped them as they neared the arch. "Wait here," he said, "and I'll prepare your way." He quickly slipped through the gate and shut it behind him before Jack could get a glimpse inside.

He stared for a moment at the black metal hinges, then reached up to crack his neck. It didn't pop the way it used to.

He looked around at the others. Millie had fallen to her knees to pluck a purple flower in the short grass beside the path. Elliott twirled a long stem of grass between his teeth and leaned a shoulder against the stones on one side of the arch. Alexis was pacing and seemed nervous as ever.

The professor removed his hat from his bald head and posed a question to them all. "So what's next, do you suppose? Somehow, I don't picture a vast throne room on the other side of that gate. Or fluffy clouds bedecked with little cherubs." There was a twinge of sourness in his tone.

Jack spoke up. "Nate called it only the entrance—the entrance to forever. Maybe that means we still have a long way to go. Till we reach the real place, that is. But who knows?"

Alexis sneered. "Count on our guide to be cryptic, all right."

Jack gazed again across the meadow to the ocean waves. His focus moved up from the shoreline to the wide blue surface stretching beyond it and onward to the far blue horizon. Then his eyes saw something they hadn't perceived before. The dim outlines of vast, bluish-green mountains rose up in the hazy distance beyond the sea. Above and beyond them were even more mountains. And above those—even more. No matter how high he looked, there were always more, in defiance of what his brain told him was physically possible.

The sound of the gate opening broke the spell of Jack's gaze. Nate came out.

"It's time," he said solemnly.

A fresh jolt of inexplicable fear passed through Jack's chest.

Slowly, they followed Nate under the archway and through the gate. The moment they stepped over the stone threshold, a new scene exploded into view.

Impossibly, they found themselves in what was like a multiplied Grand Central Station packed with people, a vast noisy throng, swirling and alive. Jack and his companions began walking along something like a mezzanine that circled around one side of the vast hall, just above the main floor.

Below were people of all ages, races, and colors dressed in every form of clothing imaginable. Jack spotted teenagers, babies, old people, middle-aged people, all talking and laughing and shouting and moving. He could see people in peasant rags as well as business suits, in jeans as well as sarongs, in military khakis as well as medical uniforms, in the skimpy attire of tropical tribes as well as the padded garb of tundra dwellers. The variety was overwhelming.

From high arched windows, huge rays of sunlight angled downward and streamed across the surging crowds. Between the windows, along the edges of the room, what looked like elevator compartments of various bright colors were moving upward, although there were no cables or pulleys or gears that Jack could see.

He looked higher. At least a hundred yards overhead, the roof was a webwork of upsweeping arches that kept swinging and gliding under and over each other, creating openings that allowed the elevators to pass upward and beyond. As the openings shifted, they revealed various views of a vast starry sky high above, a sky that seemed studded far more thickly with stars and galaxies and planets than any night view from earth.

"*Wow!*" Elliott shouted above the throng's roar as he looked up at the fantastic ceiling. "Nate," he called, "is it daytime here or nighttime?"

"Yes," Nate answered with a laugh.

"And all these people," Elliott continued. "Are they like us?"

"They are," Nate called back. "Newcomers, and their guides."

The group moved more briskly along the mezzanine. A few hundred feet ahead of them, Jack could see one of the elevators waiting, a bright yellow one with open doors. He was sure it was for them and instantly dreaded stepping inside.

Maybe the time was finally right to approach Nate for a quick private talk. Jack moved closer behind their guide until he was at his shoulder. Up close, he could see more clearly the ugly scar below Nate's ear, marking a curve across his upper jawline.

Jack came abreast of him and spoke just loudly enough to be heard. "Nate, I'd like to ask you something."

"Please do," Nate replied warmly, without slowing his pace.

"I'm a little apprehensive about…about going into God's presence, as you put it."

Nate's response was swift. "Being in his presence is what God created you for, Jack. On earth as well as in eternity."

"So…does that mean I'm wrong to feel edgy about this? I mean, I'm not exactly a religious guy. This is all new to me. Is it foolish for me to be so nervous? About what's coming next?"

"No," Nate answered clearly. He stared into Jack's eyes and offered no more.

Jack swallowed hard, craving an explanation, but Nate's look intensified his dread. He dropped back with the others.

They promptly drew near the yellow elevator with the open doors. Without a word, Nate motioned them in. Millie stepped aboard, with Elliott right behind.

"Wait a minute!" Alexis shouted above the noise still swelling up from the crowd below. "What is this thing? Where's it taking us?" Jack and the professor stood beside her.

"I'll explain inside," Nate told them. He stood next to the door with his burly arms crossed. He wasn't smiling.

The clamor of the multitude suddenly grew even louder, rising to an almost deafening pitch. Jack almost reached up to cover his ears.

With a look of alarm, Alexis glanced back and forth from Jack to the professor, trying to say something.

"What?" Jack shouted. The professor lowered his head and cupped his hand to his ear.

As the noise built to a crescendo, Alexis looked from one of them to the other, frantically trying to communicate, but she was speaking too rapidly for Jack to read her lips. She stomped her heel in exasperation.

Jack and the professor exchanged glances, then they each took one of her arms and guided her inside. Alexis didn't resist them. Nate stepped in right behind them, and the doors quickly closed, totally blocking the sound from the outside. At once, they felt the elevator's upward movement.

The compartment seemed much bigger from the inside. The metal walls and floor and low ceiling were a dull gold color. Jack looked behind him. He couldn't even tell where the doors had been. It was as though they had disappeared altogether. There were no buttons or levers inside.

With her head bowed, Alexis had her back pressed against one of the walls and was holding one hand over her eyes and cupping her elbow with the other.

The professor took off his hat and held it at his side. "Well," he said to Nate, "may we kindly hear that explanation you promised?"

Alexis dropped her hand from her eyes and joined the professor in staring at their guide.

Nate stood with his upraised palm resting on the metal wall. His face showed a sadness that Jack hadn't detected there before. He nodded and opened his mouth. "We'll be—"

"It's a trap!" Alexis snapped. "I don't care what you say about joy and pleasure and God, it's a lie. It's all a trap. And I want you to know I hate being here! I *hate* this!" She sobbed and covered her eyes again.

Nate waited a moment, then began once more. "We'll be making a couple of stops. At the first one, you'll get out, and you'll have the opportunity to reexperience certain moments from your life on earth. We'll stay there as long as you want. I'll be waiting here at the elevator when you're ready to move on."

His words seemed to relax the situation and make every-body grow reflective. Alexis regained her composure, and they all were quiet, apparently lost in their own thoughts.

The ride seemed a long one. Now and then, Jack felt a slight swaying in the elevator's movement. He looked around. No one was making eye contact, as if they were all strangers in an elevator on earth.

Finally, they felt a pull as the elevator slowed to a stop. The doors opened—on a different side of the compartment than before. A silvery light beckoned them out, and they all stepped toward it.

Nate stopped a couple of steps from the door. "Remember," he called, "I'll be here when you're ready to go."

Immediately ahead of them was a wide arching bridge made of some clear substance, almost like the crystal barrier, but not as bright. Side by side the five travelers moved up the bridge's span.

When they reached the top, the silvery overcast above them was transformed. Jack saw that the bridge was inside a giant translucent sphere.

The sphere's surface began to move and glow with color. At first, the colors formed abstract forms and unrecognizable pictures, with shades and hues and tones always in flux. Light shimmered through the colors as they danced on the dome overhead.

Jack was breathless, mesmerized. He kept turning to see the pulsing sights all around him. Suddenly, he lost his footing and felt himself slipping from the bridge, but instead of falling, he floated in the air, just as he'd done above the coffee shop patio after the accident.

He looked back to the bridge and saw the other travelers staring in various directions, enraptured by their own experiences. Jack wondered what they were seeing.

Millie was nearest to him. She was staring up in wide-eyed wonder. Jack moved toward her, and she saw him coming. She grabbed his arm and pulled him closer.

"Look!" she shouted and pointed. "That's my dog Skipper!" A golden retriever bounded before them before fading from sight. Millie giggled with sheer delight. "I was just a little girl then," she said.

Another floating blur suddenly flickered and snapped to life, as if waiting for a cue. The picture was of an old, unpainted clapboard house.

"Ohh, my!" Millie said with a nostalgic moan. "Our house! I do believe I'm seeing the house I grew up in..."

Millie

III≡

The fully three-dimensional images on the sphere seemed so real. Looking at Millie's house, Jack felt as if he were there—not watching, but actually there. He could even feel cold air—it had to be wintertime. A dog barked in the distance.

Millie seemed almost to be directing the images with her thoughts as the view zoomed up the front-porch steps and on through the front door.

Inside, a lime-green sofa rested on a frayed burgundy rug at the center of the room. Around the room's upper edges, drab tan wallpaper was peeling off, revealing bare pine planking identical to the floor. Jack could feel a bit of heat radiating from a coal stove in one corner, though the room was still mostly chilly.

On one side, a bare-board staircase ascended to the upper story. Beside it, on an overturned milk crate in the corner, sat a metal coal bucket with a scraggly pine tree sticking out of it. On the floor beside it was a closed shoe box.

Her eyes shining, Millie took in every detail of the tiny room. "Oh, I know what day this has to be," she told Jack. "And I remember what's to happen next."

The only sound was the shrill whistling of a teakettle, which seemed to come from an adjacent room through a doorway beside the stove. The whistling ended, and Jack heard low voices. Jack thought he smelled cornbread, and maybe peanut butter, mingled with the pervasive smells of coal smoke and pine.

From the next room, a man walked in holding a china cup. Jack heard a little gasp of delight from Millie as she watched him.

The man took a sip, then set his cup down on the milk crate beside the bucket with the tree in it. That's when Jack noticed one small box sitting beneath the tree. It was wrapped in newspaper and tied with yellow ribbon.

Jack guessed the man was in his mid-forties. He wore faded denim overalls and a brown flannel shirt with threadbare elbows. He got down on one knee, took the lid off the shoe box, and one at a time pulled out small, shiny glass balls—red and green and gold and silver, just two or three of each color. He worked carefully as he hung them by their package-twine loops on the tree, looking unsure whether his rough hands were up to such a delicate task.

Millie seemed breathless until he finished. But not one ball was dropped or broken.

The man's timing was perfect. Just as he put the lid back on the shoe box, the patter of feet sounded on the ceiling above him. He walked over to the stairs as a little barefoot girl—maybe four, or five at most—hurried down them. She was dressed in a faded pink nightgown and a blue sweater peppered with holes.

"Mornin', Millie!" the man called with mock surprise as she jumped from the fifth step into his arms. "Who let the angel out?"

"Daddy!" she squealed as he spun her around. As he hugged her tight, she looked over his shoulder at the Christmas tree, her eyes bright.

Just then a woman wearing a black sweater and an apron over her blue-checked skirt appeared in the doorway. Wrapping her hands in the folds of her apron, she smiled on the scene.

Jack heard the barest whisper from the older Millie beside him: *"Hello, Momma!"*

The man carried the little girl over to the tree and held her there. She reached out a finger and lightly tapped a shiny green ball, making it dance.

"Daddy?" she said.

"Yes, baby?"

"Can I open my present?"

"Of course you can, baby, but now what did we talk about just last night? What is it I said we should do first?"

The child's eyes were glued to the gift beneath the tree. "I forgot," she said.

Standing beside Jack, the older Millie giggled in embarrassment. "Oh my, wasn't I a naughty, selfish child?"

Jack winced and shook his head at her with a smile.

Little Millie's father pretended shock. "You *what?*"

She tilted her little head in dismay and answered in a smaller voice, "I forgot."

He coaxed her. "You forgot so *fast?* But surely it's not possible my little angel could forget so fast about the best present ever?"

"I remember, I remember!" the little girl squealed, looking her father square in the face and pressing her hands to his cheeks.

"You *do?*"

"I do!"

"You *sure?*" he teased.

"Daddy, I do, I do remember!"

"All right, what is it?"

"It's something I want to tell you about."

"Then, girl, I want to hear it!" He let her down from his arms and sat on the sofa. She curled in his lap and called for her momma to join them. The woman in the doorway came and sat down and snuggled beside them as they all gazed admiringly at their Christmas tree.

Standing beside Jack, the older Millie pressed his arm and whispered, "Oh, and I know what's to happen next. This is a day I never forgot."

As Jack smiled and looked at her, he noticed Elliott coming to join them. Millie saw the young man, too, and reached for his arm to pull him near so that she was flanked by him and Jack. This was obviously a moment she wanted to share.

"Is this from your childhood, Millie?" Elliott asked, taking in the scene before them.

"My fifth Christmas, I think it was," she answered. "Yes, nineteen forty-four. And no Christmas could be better, though I had so many, many good ones still to come."

"And who's that in the picture by the stairs?" Elliott asked.

Jack hadn't noticed it before. On the wall beside the stairway was a framed photograph of a serviceman in uniform.

"That's Curtis, my only brother," Millie answered. "Thirteen years older. And just a month before, on the day before Thanksgiving, we found out he'd been killed in France." Her voice was breaking. "And now it's so very soon that I finally get to see my big brother again—and Daddy and Momma, too."

On the sofa in the little room, the little girl's mother spoke up. "So now what's this you're gonna tell us, Millie honey?"

"About the best present ever."

"And what could that be?" her father asked. She pressed against his chest, and he gently rested his chin on her head.

"Jesus."

"Jesus? And why would that be?"

"Because."

"Because why?"

She squinted her eyes in concentration. "Because 'God

so loved the world, that he gave his only begotten Son, that whosoever believeth in him should not perish, but have everlasting life.'"

"You mean—God gave us *that?*" her father asked.

She slowly nodded.

"For you and me and Momma?"

She smiled and nodded again.

"And Curtis…and the whole world, too?"

Little Millie pointed to the picture of her brother.

"Yes he did, for all of us."

The three were silent for a while, still looking at the spindly pine tree with the shiny little colored balls. Tears formed in the man's eyes. The little girl sensed something wrong and looked up at him.

"Daddy, why are you crying again?"

He squeezed her tight in his arms. "Millie girl," he said, "I expect you're not entirely sure what all those words mean. About God giving his Son and all. Am I right about that?"

"Yes, Daddy."

"Well, I promise you, darlin', that even as you keep getting older, I'll never stop explaining it to you the best I know how."

The little girl rested her head on his chest once more.

"He kept that promise, too," the older Millie said quietly. "And it was the best present he ever gave me." Elliott squeezed his arm around the old woman's shoulder. "Thank you, oh, thank you," Millie whispered, looking upward again.

Jack wondered what it all meant.

The scene from the little room blurred and faded.

The next image swam into focus with a wave of sultry heat. Jack saw a small room with plank flooring and walls and open rafters. Inside, a few dozen people sat on rows of wooden benches with no backs. Their clothing—white shirts for most of the men and pastel dresses for the women—contrasted vividly with their black skin.

No hint of a breeze came from the open, unscreened windows on each side—quarter-pane windows set in unpainted frames, with no curtains or shades. The room exuded an aroma of perspiration.

On a post-leg table in front of the benches, a foot-high rough wooden cross stood alone on a crisp white tablecloth. Beside the table stood Millie's father.

Jack turned to look at Millie beside him. Her eyes glowed with pride. "Our little church couldn't afford a pastor," she explained to Jack and Elliott, "so my daddy preached there almost every Sunday till the day he died."

Her father was the only man in the room wearing a coat, a pale blue suit jacket. He looked older and thinner than he had in the Christmas scene, and his hair showed a touch of gray.

With upturned face and closed eyes, he had his Bible tucked under his arm, with the other hand extended palm outward toward the bowed heads of the people.

"Looks like it's about over," Millie said. "He would always pray like that at the end."

His outstretched arm shifted directions as he prayed for various individuals by name, asking God's help in a variety of ways—tranquility for a child troubled by bad dreams, healing for a woman's broken arm, wisdom for a father with a wayward son, money to pay a doctor's bill. The voice was deep, weighted with compassion. Jack felt soothed and comforted by the words—in spite of himself.

"Amen." The deep, hushed word on the man's lips announced the prayer's close. He opened his eyes and called loudly, "*Amen!*"

At once an older man with snow-white hair stood up in the front row and raised a hand. "Brother Wright!" he called.

A little startled, Millie's father acknowledged him. "Yes, Brother Saddler, what is it?"

Beside Jack, Millie threw a hand to her cheek in a burst of recognition. "Just what I suspected," she told her companions. "Watch now!"

Brother Saddler flashed a grin over his shoulder at his fellow worshipers, then addressed the man before them. "We have a surprise for you."

"How's that, sir?"

"Well, this is how it is: You're always doing us so much good, Brother Wright, but hardly standin' still to listen when we try to say thank-you. So now we have something good to pass along to you, something you can't refuse. However," he added, wagging his finger, "we're telling you ahead of time that you only get to enjoy this gift a few days. That's all! After that—you got to send it back."

The congregation chuckled in their shared knowledge of the riddle, while the expression of puzzlement only deepened on the face of Millie's father.

The older man pointed to a door in the room's far corner beyond the table and the cross. "You best go and open that door," he said. "Cause I think something's there you'll be mighty pleased to lay your eyes on."

Millie's father looked only briefly at the door behind him, then turned back with confusion.

"Well, well now," Brother Saddler said, shaking his head as he stepped toward the door. "I suppose I'll have to open it myself!"

When he reached the door, he turned the black metal knob, then stepped back and pulled it open.

In the doorway, in a military skirt and uniform, stood Millie as a young woman. "I'm home, Daddy!" she said. "Five days' leave! And all these folks paid my way to come see you."

While the little congregation laughed and applauded— and a few dabbed at their eyes with handkerchiefs—the pastor wasted no further time, rushing to his daughter with open arms, drawing her close in his embrace.

Another scene, filled with green, popped into view. They seemed to be hovering above jungle-covered hills. In a clearing, they could see what looked like a military camp with huge green tents surrounding an open area where a helicopter rested. One of the tents bore a big red cross on top. Soldiers were carrying a loaded stretcher from the helicopter to the medical tent.

As the scene came into focus, Alexis stepped forward to join the others. "This looks like Vietnam," she said.

"Not far from Pleiku," Millie said. Her voice seemed emotionless and distant. "I was a nurse in the army, mostly at Fort Benning in Georgia until the mid-sixties, but I reenlisted and volunteered for Vietnam when the war worsened over there."

Their view moved inside the medical tent, where harried medics rushed around to prepare a surgery table. Behind them, men with bloodied bandages occupied half a dozen cots. One or two groaned aloud. The air was heavy with heat and humidity and the odors of sweat and medicine.

The focus narrowed tightly to one of the cots, where a woman worked hurriedly to clean gaping wounds in a young soldier's arm and shoulder and neck. The man's eyes flashed fear, and he began tossing his head. She reached up and calmly pressed his cheek and smiled at him, and he relaxed.

"You'll be fine," she said.

"Do I…get to keep my arm?"

"Umm…which one?" she joked.

He groaned and grinned.

"You're okay," she said firmly as she tightened a tourniquet.

"I hope so," he answered in a raspy voice. "You know, today's my birthday."

She laughed aloud. "You're kidding! It's mine, too!"

That brought a momentary smile to his troubled face. "Nineteen for me."

"Well, don't you dare let anyone here know it," she said in a fierce whisper, "but it's twenty-six for me."

"No…can't be," he said.

"Uh-huh." She nodded.

The nurse kept working, glancing over now and then at the surgery table. In the background came the sounds of orders being yelled and the groans of the wounded.

"Birthdays," the young soldier said, struggling to stay coherent. "They're…they're for getting things, not losing things, you know. Like an arm."

"Oh, you're so right," she nodded. "Let's keep it that way." She was pressing on his shoulder wound, trying to stanch the bleeding. He winced.

He turned to stare into her eyes and spoke with quick breaths. "Hap…happy birthday."

The nurse returned his gaze. "What's your name, soldier?"

"Larry."

She smiled her biggest smile. "Happy birthday, Larry. You're going to be fine."

At that moment, a strange shrieking noise sounded over the scene. The nurse bent over the soldier, shielding his body, her expression locked in terror. Then came a blinding flash and the sound of an explosion. Roils of smoke dimmed the scene, and Jack heard people screaming. He was reminded of the coffee shop.

The next thing they saw was Millie spread unconscious on the debris-littered ground some distance away, her clothes blackened and her legs mangled and twisted. It was easy to see she would never walk again. Voices yelled in the distance.

Jack longed to run out and help her, but knew he couldn't.

The smoke billowed thicker, completely blocking their view.

In that moment, Jack was hit with a vivid memory of his own. With a sharp pang, he remembered how he'd treated Millie in the coffee shop as he passed by her wheelchair on his way out to the patio. She'd called a greeting to him…and he had deliberately snubbed her.

That seemingly insignificant moment suddenly seemed to Jack to be the truest revelation of his character, the unmistakable picture of what kind of person he actually was.

It showed what kind of person Millie was, too. She had every right to be irritated with him when he jostled her wheelchair trying to get by; instead, she cheerfully wished him a good day. Jack could still hear her words. At the time she spoke them, they had annoyed him, and he'd inwardly told himself that she was only being sarcastic, which justified his ignoring her. Why had he been so self-absorbed?

He had ignored her. She'd been friendly, and he'd been a jerk. He, a man with two good legs, had turned his back on her in disrespect, engrossed with himself. A woman who'd spent nearly forty years in a wheelchair, a woman wounded and crippled in service to her country, had reached out to him in kindness, when she had every right to be bitter.

"Were you angry?" a voice called. It was Alexis, asking Millie. But she was talking about Vietnam, not the coffee shop.

"Angry at who?" Millie replied, watching the smoky scene dissolve.

"At…at God. For taking your legs."

"Oh, but child!" Millie answered. "Haven't you seen me up here?" She laughed uproariously and gave some chorus-line kicks as she sang, "I got legs! You got legs! All God's children got legs!"

"But Millie!" Alexis whined. "You had to spend almost a whole lifetime without them!"

Millie chuckled again to herself and did a little two-step, as if the issue was now empty of any concern to her. "You know, child," she said, "I just may never stop dancing!" She grabbed Elliott's hand and shoulder and let him whirl her away in something like a waltz as they both laughed hysterically.

That left Jack alone with Alexis, gazing after the duo dancing into empty space.

"Okay, I accept it," Alexis muttered. "I accept her happiness. And I can be happy for her. But some of us in life lost something greater than our legs." She looked at Jack, almost with accusation. "And we never got it back," she added bitterly.

Jack felt a spinning sensation and looked up. Around them, the sphere's images flashed with lightning speed in a rotating movement that made him dizzy. Then the movement slowed.

They were in another place, at another time.

Alexis

≡

N o. Please, no," Alexis whispered. "I don't want to see this." But she watched closely, and so did Jack.

On a grass-covered hillside they saw another little girl of four or five. She had blond hair and wore a bright blue play outfit and was lying on her back in the grass, watching clouds overhead. A church steeple rose close by, with rooftops of houses farther in the distance.

The girl pointed upward. "Look! That one!" she said aloud, seemingly to no one. "It looks like...like an elephant! There's his trunk, and there's his big legs. And his big floppy ear."

"And over there!" she said excitedly. "A squirrel! The elephant is looking at a giant squirrel. Look at his tail!" She was forming the shapes with her finger.

"Can you please move them closer together?" she asked in a genuine plea. "I think they want to play."

A shadow appeared. Someone was walking toward the

girl—a young man in a sweatshirt. Jack placed him in his early twenties.

"Hi, Lexie!" he called as he came closer. "Who the heck were you talking to?"

She sat up, a little embarrassed, and lowered her head in her folded arms for a moment. She answered in a muffled voice. "I dunno."

"Come on," he laughed. "Can't you tell me?"

She plucked blades of grass as she thought about her answer. "I was talking to God," she admitted. "About his clouds."

"Yeah?" He looked into the sky.

"You told us that in Sunday school—to talk to him. Because he's real."

"Wow, that's right. And I thought none of you kids were listening!" He reached down and lightly tousled her hair. "I'm proud of you, Lexie. And when they let me teach your class again, I'll tell you lots more about God."

He hurried away, pausing once to call back to her. "Hey, I just left the pastor's office, and heard the ladies stepping out of their meeting down the hall. Your mom's probably looking for you."

Her eyes followed him till he was out of sight, then she leaped to her feet and romped down the hill toward the church.

It appeared to be a happy scene, but when Jack turned to Alexis, her face seemed steeled in hurt, her jaw stiff with resentment.

The picture folded in on itself and reopened to another image.

In a dark sky, the same church steeple pointed heavenward, lit by spotlights from its base.

In the foreground a single car sat in an asphalt parking lot—a 1984 Pontiac Firebird. Jack knew his cars. Looking intently into the scene, Jack could feel the cool evening air. A single streetlamp was shining nearby.

Slowly the picture's focus narrowed in on the car, its windows rolled halfway down. Sitting behind the steering wheel was the same man Jack had seen on the hillside, looking somewhat older. A pretty teenage girl, maybe sixteen, sat next to him.

"You'll see, Lexie," he was telling her. "It'll all smooth out. Just give your friends some time."

She smiled and gave an eager nod. "I should go now, I guess," she told him. "I know I shouldn't have waited for you here like this. But I had to talk it out right away—with somebody. I couldn't wait."

"Sure. I understand."

She put her hand on the door handle at her side. "Thank you for listening, Thomas."

He shifted his shoulders toward her, and rested an elbow on the steering wheel. "Any time, Lexie, you know that."

"Yeah. It…it seems like I don't really trust anybody the way I feel like trusting you."

"You *can* trust me, Lexie. Always. I promise you that."

Her brow was furrowed. She let go of the door handle. "I think…I think I trust you because I know you always pray about things."

Thomas answered only with a quick smile. Then his smile faded. He began raising his right hand toward her, then let it drop. "One thing, Lexie, that I find myself wanting to pray a lot about…is you."

She blushed, saying nothing.

He raised his hand again and slowly rested it on her shoulder.

Her blush deepened. Her neck tensed. "I…I don't know about this," she said. She slowly turned to look out her window, reaching again for the door latch.

He moved his hand to her neck, rubbing it gently.

"I just don't know," she said again.

"You can trust me, Lexie. It's okay."

Her face was still turned away. "But I don't understand. I mean, God…"

"God understands," Thomas whispered. "It's fine, Lexie."

She closed her eyes.

"It's all okay," he told her again.

He massaged her neck and shoulders for a long time. With his left hand he unbuckled his belt, then reached over to gently stroke her cheek. He used his palm to slowly turn her face in his direction. His right hand tightened on her shoulder as he pulled her to him.

The scene ended, the parking lot and the steeple and the Firebird all flickering away like the switch of a television channel.

Jack looked beside him at Alexis. Her expression was one of rigid, impenetrable coldness. Jack wanted to call out the question: *How could God let that happen?*

The new scene was a dining room. Jack recognized the teenaged Lexie seated at the table, wearing a honey-colored turtleneck and a gold cross and chain around her neck. Thomas sat across from her, wearing a navy sweater. An older man in a shirt and tie sat at the head of the table, and a woman was just placing a serving bowl on the table before sitting down as well. *Her parents*, Jack guessed.

"Lexie," her father said, "can you please pass me the rice?"

As she silently handed it to him, he said softly, "Lexie, are you all right? You look flushed. And you've hardly touched your food." He turned to his wife. "Lexie's ill."

"No, Mom, Dad, I'm fine," Lexie protested. "Just tired. Really, that's all." She had a vacant expression.

Her mother said to their guest, "Must be those late-night prayer meetings you're having for the youth. Not that it isn't good for every one of them. How many did you say were there last night?"

"About a dozen," he replied. "Pretty good for a Saturday night. We all know there's plenty to lure them off from coming to church to pray." As he spoke, Lexie never looked at him.

"Well, Thomas," her father said, "I want to thank you again for joining us. I always love hearing you talk about what you're trying to accomplish with our young people."

Thomas nodded his appreciation.

"Especially your focus on integrity," her father continued. "I mean, we just don't hear enough about integrity any more. Really living out what we believe, every moment, day or night."

"It's just walking the talk," Thomas agreed. "Just walking the talk."

"*Hypocrite!*" a voice called. Jack looked up. It was the professor, who'd come close to stand beside Alexis and watch the scene.

The dining room scene continued playing out before them as Thomas conversed with Lexie's parents, but the sound faded away. Alexis stared at the view and spoke almost in a monotone. "I trusted you," she said. "I was just a girl, and I trusted you."

The dining room scene changed to what looked like a college dorm room. On a desk in the background piled with books, a crime show was blaring on a portable TV.

Lexie, wearing a baggy sweatshirt and jeans, sat on her bed with legs crossed and arms folded around a closed textbook. Another girl in a bathrobe was nestled in a beanbag on the floor, drinking coffee and talking.

"Alexis, I'm sure you'd have a good time with us. You'd love everybody there. Come with me and try it just once."

"I'm glad you like it, Stephanie, I honestly am. But it's not for me. Not interested."

Stephanie cocked her head. "Can I ask why? Has something happened? I mean, you told me you used to go to church all the time."

"It was a phase for me, Steph. Not anymore. And to be frank, I can't stand Christians."

"Alexis! *I'm* a Christian!"

"I don't mean you. I mean most Christians. I've learned how hurtful and mean they can be, down deep—lots of them, anyway. And besides, I've got a goal in life that they can't help me with."

"Becoming a lawyer?"

"More than that. Becoming a lawyer with a passion to put away the bad guys." She pointed her finger like a gun, and "fired" it.

The moment she did, another scene popped into view before them.

It was a vast, high-ceilinged room lined with sturdy shelves filled with endless multi-volume sets of reference books. The college student Alexis sat at one of several oak tables, with a short stack of books at her elbow. Seated with her, to Jack's surprise, was the professor, wearing a rumpled tweed jacket.

"So if I heard you right," she was saying quietly as she leaned forward, "God is only who we make him to be. It doesn't matter how we worship or who we worship, or even *if* we worship."

"More or less," the professor answered. For an instant, he appeared slightly uncomfortable. "Actually I just threw that out for you to think about. I can't answer all your questions, Alexis. My job is simply to help you clarify the real issues so you can find the answers yourself. And the ultimate issue is to decide for yourself who God is. It's a highly personal decision that has to be based on your own life experiences."

"Then I've decided," Alexis said flatly, sitting up straight in her chair. "I've made up my mind."

"Oh? And what's your decision?"

"God is nothing. Nothing at all. And I want nothing more to do with talking about it." She stood to go, pulling a ski parka from her chairback and slipping it over her shoulders. "Gotta run to class. But thank you so much for meeting me here." She shook his hand, picked up her books, and hurried out the door.

"And I was right," Alexis said, standing next to Jack and the professor. "It was a careful, reasonable, thought-out decision, and it was right for me, I know it. It was right according to my experience and the best of my understanding and my integrity." There was defensiveness in her tone, as she looked at the professor. "I have nothing to be ashamed of. I have no regrets. There was no way I could have made any other decision."

"Yes, Alexis, yes," the professor was saying. "I understand that well, but it's possible—"

"Don't say it," she said curtly. "Nothing more. I'm

through here, and I don't want to see any more or hear any more."

She briskly walked away.

The professor looked ready to call out to her, but just then a beam of red light came from somewhere deep in the wall of the sphere, transfixing Jack's attention.

The Professor

|||≡

The end of the bright red light beam was just a dot, no bigger than the end of a pencil, but extremely bright. As Jack watched, the space around the light began to change. Other colors and shapes began to appear and to shift in and out of focus. The space around the red light began to swim. It surrounded them, enveloping them in a new picture.

It was a classroom, and Jack found himself staring at a map of Europe. A bright, red dot was fixed on a point in southern Germany. It came from a laser pointer in the hand of the professor, standing in front of his students. Behind him, handwritten in the upper corner of a marker board, were the words "Sean Stafford / Philosophy 112."

"In those years of wandering around Europe," the professor lectured, "Friedrich Nietzsche published the story of the madman coming down from the mountain with his lantern lit in broad daylight. He came to enlighten the people in the village, and he cried out, 'God is dead! God is dead and remains dead,' and we have killed him!' After the people laughed at these words, the madman threw his lantern to the ground, breaking it and putting out the light."

The professor paused, held up a small Bible, then tossed it onto the floor.

"So what do you think?" he continued. "Isn't that basically what we've done in our culture? Haven't we murdered God?"

Jack thought again about the little church of his childhood, the fragrance of baked beans and fried chicken and the ladies unwrapping their hot dishes in the basement kitchen. Is that what they'd been doing back there—trying to keep God alive?

The picture changed again.

They were inside a small pub, and the professor sat at a corner table with several other men who also looked like professor types. The table was littered with beer mugs and glasses, most of them empty.

Despite the loud talking and background laughter in the crowded room, the men at the table seemed engaged in an intense discussion. Jack strained his ears to hear.

"But think again of Kierkegaard's reasoning in *Fear and Trembling*," the professor was telling his colleagues. "It's hard to see if there needs to be any God at all. The choice of faith isn't a real choice. It's something we make up out of despair—a leap in the dark with nothing to land on."

A low grumble came from across the table, growing to a verbal challenge: "But, Stafford, you still aren't answering the question. Can theology as we know it sustain any true correlation to proven reality?"

As the professor gathered his thoughts for a reply, a sympathetic comrade next to him bought him some time by jabbing his finger at the questioner across the table. "Nor, Jenkins, have *you* adequately answered *my* earlier question, which is this: What point is proven by the fact that existentialism produces not only frequent suicide, but habitual Friday night drunkenness? *Bartender!*" he yelled. "Another round for this table!" The band of academic brothers laughed heartily.

Jack turned to the man standing at his side watching this. Instead of humor, the professor's eyes were filled with haunting uncertainty.

The scene before them fast-forwarded.

Jack watched as the professor walked out the door of the pub and headed down the street. He moved slowly, his hands in his pockets. He kept his eyes on the ground. After a couple of blocks, he turned a corner, then checked his watch. He picked up his pace.

A few more blocks brought him to a gray stone church, small and very old. Soft light shone from its arched amber-glass windows. The professor made his way to the red double doors under a carved inscription that read SAINT MATTHEW'S. On one of the doors, a sign announced in block letters: "Weekly Vigil—Midnight Friday."

The professor looked up and down the street before venturing in.

About a dozen people were scattered among the pews inside the candlelit chapel. Most were silent; a few whispered their prayers.

The professor took a seat in a pew near the back, pulled down the foldout padded kneeler, and dropped to his knees.

Jack was close enough to hear his barely whispered words: "I want to believe. I want to believe! I know you aren't dead, God, and I want to believe. Please, God, help me. I want to know the truth once and for all."

"Is that the *real* you, professor? A real *prayer?*" The question came from a young man's voice.

Startled, Jack and the professor turned around to see Elliott.

The professor answered dejectedly, "I suspect it was as real as I knew how to make it. But maybe not real enough for God."

Elliott placed a firm hand on the professor's shoulder. "Well," he said, "don't go selling God short."

Abruptly, the chapel walls before them began to move and expand, stretching, distorting. The amber windows became reflective, showing distorted images and shapes like circus mirrors. The whole jumbled display transformed into something different yet again.

"*Hey!*" Elliott roared as he observed the new scene. "That's *me!*"

Elliott

III≡

In a perfect match with Elliott's personality, the next images came in rapid-fire succession—a stream of highlights from his life.

A toddler jumping from a sofa onto a pile of blankets.

A boy in climbing gear hanging next to his dad on a rock formation.

An older boy with an oar in his hands and white water spraying his face.

A teenager adjusting his goggles, then letting loose down a mountainside on a snowboard.

Then Jack, with Elliott and the professor beside him, saw some quite different images unfold.

Elliott sitting at his computer, staring, typing, looking, thinking.

Elliott and a few friends talking together in a coffee shop.

And then, unexpectedly, Elliott in a suit and tie sitting

with someone in a plush business office, with skyscraper tops in view from the window behind them.

"Whoa," Jack said, "what's that all about?"

"I got lucky," Elliott answered. "Or so I thought. In college I had an idea for an Internet operation, and it turned out to be a good one. A hot IPO on the New York Stock Exchange. A twenty-year-old turns into a millionaire."

"That happened to *you?*"

"It did," he said softly.

Jack was floored.

More images, throbbing with energy: Elliott skydiving. Surfing. Hang gliding. Diving into a school of sharks, feeding them with his bare hands. (They watched this one from *under* the water with him.)

Then came a stream of images of Elliott partying, dancing, drinking. And flaunting his cash.

"Man, Elliott. You had it all."

"No I didn't. I *tried* it all. But all I ever really *had* was flat-out nothing."

The throbbing party images seemed nonstop. Lots more drinking. Shooting up. Making out.

"So maybe you got a little wild at times," Jack commented. "But do you really call that *nothing?*"

"It's nothing when you've got a hole inside you and everything you frantically cram into it just drains out faster and faster, leaving you emptier than ever."

Suddenly the frenetic pace of the images ground to a halt.

A moonlit mountain trail high above timberline drew their gaze. They felt the chill of night air. Someone walked slowly up the trail. Elliott? Yes, but all they could see was his back. His slowness seemed less the exhaustion of a hiker than the weariness of a man locked in some intense mental struggle.

The trail hooked a switchback, but the hiker didn't follow it. He left the trail and clambered across some boulders, then came to an abrupt drop-off. The full moon illuminated a plunge of several hundred feet. Jagged rock shadows far below contrasted with the silvery light shimmering on the rock cliffs all around. He lay down at the rim, peering over the edge.

"Ten of us," Elliott said in a hollow voice. "Ten of us went up to party on the lower parts of this mountain the night before—even though I'd decided I didn't really want to do it this time. But then, there was nothing else I could think of worth filling the time with.

"We backpacked all our booze and drugs and not much else. But that night around the fire, something set me in a rage, and one of the guys there kept provoking it. I finally lit into him. He was so wasted he didn't have a chance. I was hammering him. It was total rage. I swore I was going to beat his head on a rock and roll him in the fire and hold him there. And that's exactly what I intended to do. But before I got to the fire, they jumped me, all eight of the others, and it took all eight to get me off him. Otherwise…I would have killed him.

"They carried him off as they all packed up and left me. I'd already gone away on my own. I kept walking aimlessly in the moonlight till dawn. Then I found a quiet place by a stream and just lay there, thinking. I slept a little, off and on, but mostly I just lay there, listening to the stream, watching the wind in the trees.

"My head was swimming. It was like my life passed in front of me, all the things I'd done. The kind of person I was. And I came to some conclusions. I made my plan.

"When night fell again and the moon had risen, I found the summit trail and headed up beyond timberline. I knew the trail well. I knew this spot we're looking at now."

In the image in front of them, they saw the weary hiker still lying and staring over the edge of the precipice. After several long moments, he sat up. He took off both his hiking boots and pulled out the shoestring from one of them. Then he tossed both boots over the edge and watched them fall. They were lost to sight long before they stopped dropping, and the noise they made when they hit bottom was too far away to be heard.

He took the shoestring cord and fashioned a small loop with a slipknot. He put the loop around both wrists and carefully cinched the knot tight, binding his wrists. With the fingers of his right hand, he wound the loose end of the cord around the fingers of his left.

He lay down on his back, his bound hands lying uselessly in front of him, then slowly repositioned his body parallel to the rim. Moonlight revealed his sorrowful, tear-stained face.

With slow, fraction-of-an-inch movements—and long pauses in between—he nudged himself closer and closer to the edge. Eventually, one of his shoulders was hanging in thin air.

"Why were you doing this?" the professor asked.

"Because I'd finally figured out the truth of who I really was. I was an angry, foolish, life-wasting playboy with a killer's heart—I'd proven that. I'd had every chance in the world for happiness and blown nearly every one. Darkness had overtaken me, and it was closing in tighter. At the moment, I honestly couldn't think of one good reason to keep on living—or of one single person who really cared if I lived or died and would miss me after I was gone.

"Most of all, I knew that dying was no worse than I deserved. I was guilty as hell—and that's just where I was headed.

"I lay there looking up into the night sky, knowing I was having my last living thoughts. I saw that moon and those stars, and I thought how they were all so incredibly perfect, so unbelievably beautiful and strong, yet I was so incredibly ugly and imperfect and weak. I saw that sky, so still and flawless and unchanging, and all I wanted was for it to stay that way and for stinking, defective me to just get totally out of the picture. And getting me out of the picture was something I could take care of."

"So…" the professor prodded, "why didn't you go through with it?"

"Two reasons," Elliott answered.

"First, as I lay there ready to roll over the edge, staring into the heavens…I saw a spectacular shooting star. A huge one. You know, the kind with a long smoky tail that stays lit for several seconds. Biggest one I'd ever seen. And in that second it came to me. I know this is weird—but I figured that falling star was *me* somehow, and yet not exactly me, but somebody falling *for* me, so I myself didn't have to fall. It all made sense for me at the moment, though I couldn't begin to fully explain it."

"And the second reason?" Jack asked.

"The second reason is this: Among my many other faults, I'm as big a coward as the next guy." Elliott howled with laughter, slapping the shoulders of the two men next to him. "That's the truth, guys!"

The three of them looked closely at the figure of the wrist-bound Elliott writhing at the edge of the drop-off. They saw the sustained flash of light on his face from the meteor and the stunned look in his eyes.

After a while, he carefully nudged himself back about an inch from where he'd been balanced over the edge. Then, with a violent burst of energy, he hurled himself back toward safety, rolling over in the dust and rocks, gagging and coughing from the powdery grit in his mouth and nose.

The cloud of dust seemed to rise up and obliterate the picture, making way for another scene.

In a crowd of people, Elliott was walking with a friend beside what looked like a movie poster in a showcase. Jack was stunned to see that it was identical to the billboard he'd seen after he left the hotel seminar. "The Thorn," the poster announced. And there again was the darkened image of the bleeding head of Christ.

Just as quickly as the image came, it disappeared, swallowed up by another that began to take shape.

"What was that?" the professor asked. "Where were you?"

"Well," Elliott explained, "a few days after my mountaintop experience, I ran into an old high school buddy who invited me to this Easter drama at his church—a retelling of Jesus dying and then rising from the dead. Considering what I'd just been through, I decided it might be what I needed."

The new scene opening before them showed a straight country road in a landscape of scrubby bushes and wild grass on a darkly overcast day. A black BMW Z3 convertible had pulled over on the shoulder, with no other traffic around.

The picture zoomed in, and they could see Elliott with his forehead resting on the steering wheel. He raised up, and they saw tears streaming down his face. Though his words were little more than a whisper, they could hear them clearly. "Please, God, help me. If you're real, I need you. I see what you did for me, and I want it. I accept it."

Raindrops pattered on the BMW's roof and windshield, quickly becoming a downpour. Jack could smell the fresh scent of it, washing over the landscape.

His view pulled up away from the car, soaring into the rain-filled sky, the BMW and the ribbon of country road growing smaller and smaller.

"Elliott—what did you do next?" Jack asked. "What happened to you?"

"Well...I didn't do much more right then except to say thank you. But as for what really happened to me..." Jack saw tears again in Elliott's eyes, coursing down his cheeks. "Man, it's a *miracle*. I felt his forgiveness washing me all over—like the rain. Inside out and outside in. I felt clean.

"I knew I deserved to die. I knew God had so much against me. But I also understood how Jesus took my punishment when he died." Elliott paused. "Jesus was my falling star."

Before Jack could hear more about this, he lost sight of Elliott and the professor. He felt himself being pulled away.

He found himself on the clear bridge again. Catching sight of the swirling sphere above him, he looked up and saw a hole opening up, a gap in the sphere that quickly grew larger. Through the opening he saw a room, and before the image came clearly into focus, Jack knew instinctively where he was.

Jack

||| ≡

Jack stood looking over the room for a moment, a moment that hung like a kite on the wind.

It was his childhood bedroom.

He saw his bright blue bedspread patterned with yellow rockets. The red carpet. His dresser with a missing lowest drawer. The white wicker clothes hamper with a chip in the corner where he'd kicked it. The closet door standing wide open, as usual.

Everything was just like it was when Jack was eight years old.

The walls were painted like a jungle. His mother had done it for him as a gift for his sixth birthday. There were Batman posters on the wall. Two of his colored-pencil drawings, one of a dog with a boy and one of a downtown skyscraper, were taped to the door.

On his wooden dresser was his collection of clay animal figurines, ones that his father had given him for Christmas, and that he'd painted himself. Jack ended up keeping them for years—not finally throwing them away until he was out of college. Seeing them again, he wished he had them back to keep forever.

Loud noises from downstairs broke his reverie. He heard his parents talking as they moved into the front hallway at the foot of the stairs. They spoke in insistent tones that were only too familiar.

"I'm sorry, honey, it's important work," his dad was telling his mom.

"But his games never take long," she contended, "and—"

"Not this time, honey." Then he shouted up the stairs on his way out, "Next week, champ! We'll make it up next week!" The front door slammed shut.

Instinctively, Jack turned toward the open closet door in his room and looked inside. Just beneath the handful of jackets and shirts drooping sloppily from wire hangers, huddled amid the piles of shoes and toys and balls and bats on the floor, was the crumpled figure of an eight-year-old boy in his baseball uniform.

Seeing him, Jack felt his heart being pierced. He knew the boy had heard that shouted promise from his father so many countless times.

"Dear God," the high-pitched voice called up from the cramped closet floor, "please help my daddy like me. Please. I just want him to like me."

It was odd to hear himself praying. Jack hadn't prayed in so long. *Why?*

As the boy cowered deeper in his closet refuge, Jack tried to remember the day he'd stopped believing in God, *really* believing in him. He couldn't put a finger on it. It must have happened gradually. It must have come like a tide on a Carolina beach, slowly but surely, until the beach was lost altogether. Somehow, he'd put God and his dad in the same boat: Uninterested.

He could think back to so many missed games, missed moments. Even his high school graduation. His father had worked a succession of sales jobs, none of them ever seeming to swallow any less of his time than the previous one.

Important work to do. That's what he always told Jack's mom; that's the excuse she always passed along to Jack. Yeah, sure. Important. As opposed to not important, like his son.

An instant later, the room was lost, and another picture opened in front of him.

Jack saw a twelve-year-old version of himself, again in a baseball uniform and wearing glasses. He was sitting in a yellow vinyl-covered chair at the kitchen table, gulping down a bowl of Wheaties and holding the cereal box in one hand. The box had a picture of Joe Montana on the front, and Jack was reading the story about Joe on the back.

On the refrigerator behind him, Pizza Hut magnets

were clinging to a few of the boy's recent drawings. On the counter by the range was the ceramic pig sugar bowl he'd made and painted when he was nine.

A figure walked into the room, his back momentarily blocking Jack's view of the table, and Jack felt his stomach tighten. It was his father, dressed in coat and tie. He took a bowl from a corner cupboard and banged it on the table.

Watching the scene, Jack swallowed hard.

"Hey, kiddo," his dad said, rubbing the boy's head.

"Hey, Dad," he answered quietly. For several minutes, they both ate their cereal, the father hurriedly catching up with the son.

"What's up, bucko?" his dad eventually asked as he neared the bottom of his bowl. "Why the long face?"

"Well…it's just that…well, our game is this morning. I was just hoping…"

"Aw, Jack. You know I want to be there. If I could only change my meeting, I'd be there. Next weekend, buddy. Play-off time, right? Best time to be there, what d'ya say?"

"Yeah, sure, Dad." But the boy knew next weekend would be no different.

After swallowing a last spoonful of milk, his father got up. "Sorry, champ," he said. "Gotta run."

Watching the scene, Jack felt a lump growing in his throat. With sudden determination, he moved toward the image of his father. "Wait, Dad," he called. "I need to talk to you. Please, just for a minute—don't leave! I…"

His father dropped his empty bowl in the sink and rushed out. The front door slammed again, and the scene disappeared.

In the next one, a teenage girl was sitting on the edge of a swimming pool, skimming the water with her dangling feet. It was Sydney. She was only sixteen and already flashing her unmistakable smile and deep blue eyes.

Too quickly, the picture flickered and faded. Jack's heart ached. He felt the surge of an agonized longing for her. For the first time since he died, he felt the dread that he would never see her again.

The sphere above became only a slow-swirling surface of gray, and Jack could see nothing more in it. Standing alone on the clear bridge, he guessed his share of the program was already over, even though his little part seemed pointless.

He sensed someone's presence nearby and turned. He was startled to see Nate.

"Why did we do this?" Jack asked quietly. "Why did we see these moments from our lives?"

"These words and actions and images reveal who you are," Nate calmly answered. "They reveal your view of love and of life and of God. What you see helps you make sense of your life and helps explain your choice."

"To be honest with you," Jack told him, "my life's not making any more sense to me than it did before. And I'm still basically clueless about that choice you spoke about."

"Remember," Nate said, "you can stay here longer if you want. You don't have to leave until you're ready."

"You mean—I can see more of my life?" Jack's heart leaped at the chance to see more of Sydney and maybe the kids as well. Even as he spoke his question, the sphere came alive again with another image of Sydney.

It was their honeymoon on St. Bart's. They were together in the back of a taxi, bumping down a dirt road. A reggae version of *Fools Rush In* blared and crackled from the speakers in front, and the cabbie—sporting a red and green hat—bobbed his head with the music.

In the backseat, the newlyweds looked at each other just like lovers do. He stretched his arm around her shoulders and pulled her close. He felt the softness of her hair against his face and kissed it. He reached over with his free hand and locked fingers with her playfully.

Jack had been determined back then to etch every detail of those moments into his mind. He had never been happier. *How was it possible*, he wondered, *that we could ever drift apart?*

The reggae faded away, and the jostling of the taxi ceased, but the scene stayed vividly bright. Jack's view tapered inward until he saw only Sydney's face, frozen in time. He stared at her eyes, her smile, at everything about her.

As he watched, his view of her seemed to magically become a composite portrait of her face in a hundred or a thousand different settings through the years, constantly changing like a many-faceted diamond turning slowly in the light. Every facet, every glimpse of her, was more beautiful than the last. Jack knew he was seeing more than just her physical beauty, but also a glimpse of the beauty of her heart.

"I love you, baby," Jack whispered as her image blurred through the tears in his eyes.

If Nate was right—if Jack didn't have to leave this place till he was ready—then he would stay here forever just to watch Sydney and wrap himself around the pictures of her.

Tears streamed down his face as her beauty captivated him like never before. And she was so close! If he could only hold her just once! He reached out to touch her, just to feel her hair again, but the pictures retreated from him. Everything in him cried out for just one more moment with her. As he thrust his reach even farther, the image faded away.

He collapsed to his knees in grief and buried his face in his hands. *How could I have been so blind all these years?*

He felt a hand on his shoulder. He looked up and saw Nate standing over him.

"Remember your last conversation with Sydney." It was more a command than a question, but spoken with a gentleness that Jack hadn't detected in Nate's voice before.

"I remember," Jack said, instantly recalling the phone call he'd received in the coffee shop. Just as quickly a wave of regret enveloped him. He remembered the clipped, impatient way he'd answered after seeing who the call was from. Remorse overwhelmed him—all because of that little, one-syllable, one-second, inconsiderate response to Sydney. *What was I thinking?*

He felt as if a black sword was stabbing through his heart. He dropped his face in his hands once more.

"Do you know why Sydney phoned you?" Nate asked. He still had his hand on Jack's shoulder.

Jack couldn't bear the flame of guilt he was feeling. He had to smother it somehow, or it was sure to cripple him. He raised his head, but without making eye contact with Nate. "Yes, of course I know," he shot back. "The kids. Problems with the kids."

"No. There was a deeper reason."

"What are you talking about?"

"She wanted to reconsider the divorce. That's why she called."

"That's impossible! What do you mean? How do you know?"

"Do you remember how your conversation ended?"

Jack remembered. "We were cut off. After...yes, she started to say something."

Nate put both his hands on Jack's shoulders. "Sydney had some apologies to make. And she wanted to put a hold on signing the papers. She wanted to start over. That's what she wanted to tell you."

Jack was dumbfounded—then furious. He felt cornered. "But we were *cut off*! How can that be *my* fault? Why are you accusing *me*? I don't control cell phone signals!"

Nate tightened his grip on Jack's shoulders. "Another cut-off happened first, Jack. The way you answered the call made Sydney defensive. It kept her from telling you right away what she wanted to say."

"But so what? She got over it, didn't she? You said she was about to tell me—so it has to be God's fault, not mine, that it never happened. *He* could've kept that signal from getting lost, but there's no way on earth I could."

Nate kept his cool in the face of Jack's anger. "And what if the signal hadn't been lost, Jack? If you'd heard her out, how would you have responded? At *that* moment? Were you ready to forgive her? Were you ready to postpone the divorce? Or would you have been blinded by the selfish attitudes you were holding on to?"

Jack was afraid he knew the answer only too well. "I—I don't know," he told Nate. "To tell you the truth, I'm too fired up right now to sort all this out."

Nate pressed relentlessly ahead. "Yet even after the phone call was cut off, Jack, you still had a chance to redeem the situation."

Jack had never felt so beaten up in his life. But he was tired of fighting it. His anger was crumbling. He had no idea how to counter Nate.

Nate seemed to sense Jack's helplessness. His voice was gentler than before. "Immediately after the phone call, the thought came into your mind to send flowers to Sydney."

Jack nodded.

"That thought took even you by surprise, and you immediately rejected it. But you shouldn't have. Sending flowers right then was the right thing to do for Sydney. It would have strengthened her again to tell you what she so desperately wanted you to hear. And maybe catch you in a better mood."

Jack felt his temper flaring again. "But—so what if I'd sent flowers? I'm dead now. By the time Sydney got them, it would still be too late to talk."

"Jack—if you'd decided right then to send her flowers, you would have been in a florist shop when the truck crashed, not in the coffee shop."

Jack slumped his shoulders in desperation. "Okay, Nate. Looks like you got me covered at every turn, every angle. So I just want to ask you one thing more—one little thing: Will I see Sydney again? I mean in present reality, not just in pictures from the past. Will she come to me?"

"I don't know," Nate answered.

"Why not? How can you find out? How can I find out?" Jack felt so hopeless.

"You may see her, Jack, and you may not. It all depends."

"Depends on *what?*"

"On her choice—and on yours."

There was that cryptic *choice* language again. Jack didn't feel like pursuing it further.

"So what happens next for me?" he asked.

"You don't have to move on until you're ready," Nate reiterated, releasing his hands from Jack's shoulders.

Jack got to his feet. He'd decided that more pictures of Sydney would simply be too painful to bear. But he desperately wanted a last glimpse of Judd and Maggie and Andy.

"If it's possible," he asked, trying to sound meek enough, "I'd sure like to see my kids."

At once the view on the sphere opened up again.

It was their house, downstairs in the family room, apparently quite recently. Andrew was sitting on the floor amid an assortment of Nerf footballs and Frisbees. That's what he most liked to play with Jack. But there was a scowl on Andy's face as he sat cross-legged with his chin cupped in his hands.

Maggie was in Jack's easy chair by the fireplace. On the lamp table beside it was a stack of her favorite story-books, the ones she most liked Jack to read from. She sat there alone.

At a card table set up in the back corner, Judd was quietly working on some model planes, a hobby he and Jack had recently taken up together.

"Wait," Jack said to Nate. "Shouldn't I be in this picture?"

"Shouldn't you be?" Nate echoed.

With a flash, Jack put his finger on it. This was last Saturday night, and he had promised the kids he'd spend that evening with them. But Sydney had been more confrontational than usual that day, and when Jack got a late-afternoon phone call inviting him to a poker-and-pizza night with his buddies, he seized the opportunity to escape, not even sticking around to have dinner with the family.

He still remembered Andy tugging at his pants leg as he hurried out the door.

"Daddy, you promised!"

"Next time, champ," Jack had answered in a rush. "Gotta run. Don't worry, kiddo, we'll make it up tomorrow. Give you more time to practice those throws on your own. Right, champ? What d'ya say?" But then, of course, as Jack now vividly recalled, on the following night he'd dashed off to the office to spend the evening taking care of some pressing details while the office was quiet.

The picture died away, but the memory lingered, an ache that seemed to fill his whole being. His own words kept reverberating in his brain, mingled with his father's voice saying exactly the same things: *Next time, champ...gotta run...what d'ya say, what d'ya say, what d'ya say?*

Jack wanted to shout, *But we had so many good times, too!* He wanted to see *those* moments with his kids replayed before his eyes, not the times he'd blown it. But now he was afraid to see any more. He felt defeated.

He turned to Nate. "I'm ready to go," he told him matter-of-factly.

"A couple of things first," Nate said, "just for you to think about." Jack cringed.

"First: Your Creator flooded your life with a countless number of happy moments with your family and with others.

Ask yourself, Jack, whether all this was more than you ever deserved and whether it was more than you ever took the trouble to thank God for.

"Second: Ask yourself honestly whether you truly have any right, considering your own shortcomings, to be the judge of the faults of your wife, of your children, or of any other person on earth.

"Let's go," Nate concluded. "The others are waiting for you at the elevator."

Nate

≡

Nate escorted Jack back across the clear bridge.

The other travelers waited quietly by the elevator—Millie, the professor, Alexis, and Elliott. They all had their eyes on Jack as he approached, as if he were a schoolkid returning to the classroom from the principal's office. Their gaze made him uncomfortable. How much did they really know about him?

Out of nervous habit, he looked at his watch. Still 12:46. *Imagine that.*

The doors to the yellow elevator opened, and the travelers turned to enter.

"Wait!" the professor said. "Pardon me, Nate, but there's something that's been nagging me, something that's fired my curiosity."

"What is it?" Nate asked.

"It's you," he replied. "Your story, that is. Before we leave this place, and if there's adequate time, I wonder if we might be able to learn more from that sphere about *your* past, just as all of us here have learned more about each other."

"Oh, yes," Millie agreed, "I'd love that!"

"Cool idea," Elliott said. "How about it, Nate?"

Nate appeared more than willing. "Back to the bridge, then." He nodded, as he turned on his heel to lead them there.

"If you don't mind," Alexis said crisply, "I'll just stay here." Nate barely nodded in her direction, as if such a response was something he'd long expected from her.

Jack, feeling mentally battered, wasn't eager for more revelations and exposures, but he did have his own share of curiosity about Nate's past. He followed the others to the clear bridge.

The sphere above them began churning again with light, color, and motion. A red sun appeared, hanging low over a thick sky—a wider, broader view than anything they'd seen earlier.

Silhouetted by the sun and staring into it, Nate stood at the top of the bridge's arch. A warm breeze was blowing, fluttering his tousled hair and swaying his rough robe around his calves. He looked more mysterious than ever.

The sun took on a golden hue and rose quickly over-head. Beneath its bright rays, a crowded marketplace appeared. The buildings around it looked Middle Eastern and extremely ancient.

Jack's focus centered on a young boy, brown skinned and dark haired, lurking in and among the market stalls.

Jack watched as a fruit peddler bartered strenuously with a woman carrying a crying baby. The young boy sneaked up behind them and nabbed a handful of figs from a basket only inches from the peddler's feet. The little thief crept away to a back alley, stashed his loot behind a pile of rocks, then went back for something more from another stall.

Jack and the travelers watched the little boy repeat his thievery several times.

"Is that really the young you?" Elliott asked Nate.

Nate nodded as the scene dimmed and changed. "From as far back as I can remember, I was always stealing. Always taking more and more. And by the time I reached the height of a man, there was no one I knew who was more skillful at stealing than I."

"You're—you're just a common thief?" the professor asked.

"I am Nathan the son of Ophel from the town of Kirioth in Judah. My father was a hard-working farmer, and he took good care of his wife and his children. I never had need to steal. But the thrill of it—claiming whatever I could that didn't belong to me—was a temptation I could never in my entire lifetime resist for very long."

"So you're a kleptomaniac," the professor said, almost with disdain.

Nate shrugged. "As you see it."

He continued his story. "And so it was that when I reached the height of a man, I turned my back upon my family and upon my home and my townsmen. I went to the city—to Jerusalem—to make a living by taking from others."

Under the bright sun, another ancient vista flowered into view—the crowded streets of Jerusalem, with the great temple of the Jews rising on a mount in the background.

"In the back alleys of Jerusalem," Nate continued, "I found a partner. We learned how we could often steal better by stealing together—though he and I also knew well how to steal from one another.

"We also learned how much more interesting and challenging it could be to steal from the many Roman officials and soldiers in Jerusalem—although it truly made no difference to us whether our victims were Jewish or Roman or anything else. From any and all we took coins, food, clothing—even horses and weapons. Eventually, I stole more than treasure and possessions. I stole virtue from women and dignity from men, whenever I could, in whatever way I could.

"But our time and our luck ran out. My partner and I were caught—in the dark of night in a Roman palace. And the Roman penalty for it was crucifixion."

As the Jerusalem scene before the travelers filled in with intense color, Jack saw a crowded, narrow street packed with jostling crowds. Roman soldiers on horseback and on foot were leading some kind of procession through the mob.

Close to the front, two men, almost naked, carried huge rough beams on their shoulders. Looking closer, Jack saw that one of the men was Nate—Nathan the thief. At one point he stumbled over loose stones in the street, and a mounted soldier nearby cracked a whip that caught Nathan just below the ear, spilling blood from the side of his face.

Farther behind these two came yet a third man carrying a cross. He staggered much more than Nathan or his partner did. His body was a bloodied mass of wounds, and a crown of thorns was pressed on his head. Gripped by his presence as he passed, many of the bystanders jeered and taunted. A few others, however, wailed and wept.

As Jack took it all in, he couldn't hold back the tears in his own eyes.

This scene evolved into another, on a hill just outside the city walls. Heavy menacing clouds swirled in the sky, hiding the sun.

On the top of the hill, three crosses stood, with a man nailed to each one. Jack saw the bloody, thorn-crowned man in the center—Jesus. Nathan was nailed to the cross on his right, and his partner was fastened to the cross on the left.

Jack could see the soldiers barking orders and people in the gathering crowd on the hill waving their fists and yelling. But no sound came from this scene. The only sound came from outside it—from Nate, who was on his knees and singing some kind of lamentation in a language Jack didn't understand. Elliott and Millie knelt beside him and began adding their own low murmurs of mournful song. The professor stood just a few steps behind them.

As the sky grew darker, the soldiers lit torches. Jack's

view zoomed closer to the tortured forms of Jesus and Nathan side by side on their crosses. He saw their flowing blood.

Then he saw them straining to speak to each other in short, gasping phrases.

Jack rushed over to where Nate, his guide, was kneeling and singing. Jack fell beside him. Nate stopped singing and turned to Jack with compassion and tears in his eyes.

"Nate," Jack pleaded, "I've got to know. What is Jesus telling you? What were you talking about?"

"My partner had been screaming at Jesus," Nate explained. "He wanted Jesus to do a miracle and get us all down from there before we died—if he really was God, as some people claimed. You see, both my partner and I had heard what people were saying about Jesus. We knew what Jesus was teaching.

"And there on the cross beside him, I'd been watching Jesus and listening. I saw him in a way that maybe only the dying can see him.

"So I strained for breath enough to rebuke my partner into silence. I reminded him that he and I deserved what we were receiving that day. But not Jesus. Not him. Jesus had done nothing wrong—I was sure of that.

"I turned to Jesus, and I strained for breath again. I said to him, 'Jesus, remember me when you come into your kingdom.'"

"How did Jesus answer?" Jack asked.

"In a better way than I thought possible, a way I would

never expect. He said to me, 'Truly I tell you this, that today you'll be with me in Paradise.'"

"A thief," Jack whispered. "In Paradise! How was that possible?"

"Watch the blood, Jack," Nate answered, nodding toward the image of Christ bleeding on the cross. Jack stared at him. "That blood makes it possible, Jack. It's the blood of someone who had never done anything wrong in his entire life. That blood was flowing because of all the wrong *I* had done. I, Nathan the thief. He could forgive me—he did forgive me—because he was paying my own debt to God. He paid it all."

Jack heard the professor's quiet voice behind them. "What happened next?"

"Very soon," Nate said, "the sky blackened even more."

They watched it happen. In the darkening and tighter image before them, Jack could see only the head of Christ, at times jerking upward as he struggled to gasp for breath.

"Then my ear was pierced by a scream from beside me. It was Jesus, crying out to God his Father. He was screaming his words to God—'Why have you forsaken me?' And in my soul I knew the answer. When his Father looked down at Jesus, he was seeing *me*. He was seeing *my* guilt— all our guilt—and he was crushing Jesus for it and deserting him there, leaving him all alone."

Jack watched as the battered face of Jesus turned

upward into the blackened sky. The sound came back up in the scene, and Jack could hear the wind from the stormy sky as it whistled around the crosses. Then Jesus cried out his words to God in a language Jack couldn't grasp—but the wrenching anguish of it echoed like deafening thunder.

Jack crouched down and covered his eyes. He heard mournful cries coming from beside him—from Nate and Millie and Elliott.

Jack stayed bowed, with his eyes closed, until the sounds died away.

He looked up.

The scene of Christ and the crosses and the darkened sky was gone. The sphere's form, gray and empty, appeared again all around them.

Nate stood up and, bending over, reached down and pulled the strips of rags from his feet. Jack saw the scars there from the crucifying nails.

Then Nate pulled the strips from his wrists, and they were scarred as well.

He held the strips in his clenched hands.

"At the end of that awful day," Nate said, "I awoke in Paradise—to be with him forever, just as Jesus promised. I was the very first to pass, under the grace of Jesus, into heaven."

He turned to lead them off the bridge. "It's time," Nate said. "We're ready now…for the two doors."

Two Doors

||||≡

The elevator's entrance closed once more.

The travelers again felt the heave of the initial movement upward.

And once more, fear gripped Jack.

He felt he'd been given the clearest possible picture of himself, and it was no pretty sight. Jack had been suddenly and terribly revealed to Jack.

He now fully grasped that heaven wasn't reserved for perfect people who'd done all the right things...or else it would be empty. Instead, he realized, heaven was reserved for those who'd been forgiven, plain and simple. And only the death of Jesus could make such forgiveness possible.

But that was a forgiveness Jack had never had a share in. His guilt and his shame were proof of his lack. They were the evidence of his own choices, like it or not. They were the evidence that he'd never accepted Jesus and all that Jesus had done for him. And if Jack had never accepted him—it was the same as rejecting him.

That's what would sentence him to an eternity apart from God.

Terror slammed him, more fear than he'd ever known. He glimpsed what awaited him: an absolute aloneness—forever. He was going to a place where nobody could be with him. Not Sydney or his kids, not Elliott or Nate or Millie, not anyone. He would be alone. Totally and completely and eternally alone.

And it had all been his own selfish choice.

He could bear it no longer. Jack knew what he had to do.

The elevator came to a stop, and the doors opened.

"It's time," Nate announced as he stepped through the doors. Elliott and Millie bounded after him, followed by the professor. Jack and Alexis were the last ones out.

As the doors closed behind them, the yellow elevator vanished entirely.

Fifty feet ahead, Jack saw two doors. He glanced from one to the other, then to Nate.

Nate was looking squarely at him.

"Jack, you're first. This is your choice. Behind one door, you feel the full weight of your judgment before God, and you plunge to an eternity without him, an eternity of punishment and fire.

"Behind the other, you rise to an eternity *with* God—an eternity reserved for those who've chosen Jesus, who've let *him* carry the weight of their judgment before God when he was crucified. It's an eternity of joy and indescribable pleasure and fulfillment.

"And the choice for you, Jack, has been yours alone."

Nate stepped aside.

"I choose Jesus!" Jack shouted. "That's my choice, Nate. Jesus!"

Everyone was silent and still, and Jack couldn't understand why. Nate's face was sad and unmoving. Jack looked instinctively to Millie, then to Elliott, but their faces were saddened as well.

"No, Jack," Nate told him. "You don't understand. This is not the moment when you can choose. This is the moment when the choice you've already made is revealed to you."

Jack's jaw dropped.

He heard a noise.

One of the doors had opened.

Jack wanted to back away and run, but he couldn't. He could only move forward, tugged inescapably toward that one open door. As he was pulled closer to it, he could *feel* what was beyond.

Nothing at all.

An absolute, total, and torturous nothing. A nothing so dreadful that it burned.

He could feel his heart being sucked toward the opening. It was heavy, like a crushing weight. He tried again to pull back and step away, but it was impossible. He was being pulled beyond himself, yet pulled by his very own choice.

The door grew larger as he came near it, and his view through the opening was more awfully and brutally dark than anything he'd ever imagined.

Plunging into darkness, he screamed—just as something like a great jolt of hot electricity ripped through his body. His arms and legs pulsed violently. Still in utter darkness, a searing pain, like nothing he'd ever felt, erupted in his chest.

Jack screamed again.

He waited for the awful torment, for the agony of absolute aloneness, but it never came. Instead, images and colors mixed together. His eyes blurred as he tried to focus. The sounds around him were slurred and slow as he winced in excruciating pain.

He heard voices. He opened his eyes and saw a face. Not the face of some hellish creature. Nor was it Nate's face or the face of any of his fellow travelers—or even of Jesus. It was the face of a woman in a white medical uniform, and she was shaking him and pressing on his chest.

As her face came into full focus, she eased up on the pressure, and Jack saw something like a smile on her face as she focused on his eyes.

Jack tried to lift his hands, but his arms felt too weak to move. A killer headache pounded his brain, sending jolt after jolt of piercing pain down into his back and shoulders.

He opened his mouth.

"Please don't try talking, sir," the woman pleaded. "Stay as still as you can. You're in good hands."

But there was something he absolutely had to ask.

He opened his mouth again, straining to breathe, and forced out the feeble words: "Do you...happen to know...what time it is?"

THE END

part II
—

Looking Through

Movie Man

||||≡

The scene: Early afternoon at a downtown coffee shop with an outdoor seating area. Two men with frappucinos seat themselves at a little metal table on the patio, under the warm and welcome sunshine. From the loudspeakers behind them, Bob Dylan is singing, "Hey, Mr. Tambourine Man…"

One of the men is John Bolin, author of this book. The other is Clint Z., who represents a major movie studio in Hollywood. For the past three hours—at a working brunch in a hotel suite—they've been discussing film rights for *The Two Doors of Heaven*. Now they've come here for a break.

"Thanks for the coffee, Clint," John says. "And for all the information you've walked me through so far. Not to mention your patience with all my questions. There's a ton of stuff to absorb in all this—merchandising rights, soundtrack rights, derivatives, sequels, prequels. Makes my head spin, but I'm having fun." John is carrying a small leather satchel. He sets it down at his feet, propped against the chair leg.

"You ask good questions, John. I appreciate your thoroughness—your interest in every detail. I really do."

Clint is a well-dressed thirty-something, Carrera sun-glasses under his tanned forehead. An open-collar Etro dress shirt in diagonal brown checks, with the little blue, winged horse over his heart. Iceberg slacks, crisp and white. Brown leather panama sandals on his bare feet. Everything Italian, John guesses.

"You know," John says, "you look pretty close to what I expected. The hip studio exec."

Clint tilts his head. "I hope that's not a put-down."

John grins. "Hey, I'm taking notes! My wife will want to know." He leans back with crossed arms. "So tell me the honest truth, Clint. I know you said that all your review team likes the book, and obviously your studio sees poten-tial in it. But I want to hear your own personal opinion."

Clint gazes out to the street as he answers. "I read every word of it. And I don't usually do that." He turns again to John. "Does that tell you something?"

John nods slowly. "It does."

Clint glances around him. "You said you like coming here to write. Was it here that you first got the idea for the book?"

"Parts of it, yeah. Actually, the original idea goes back a year ago, when I received a call that Papu, my grandfather in Nebraska, had died in his sleep. I felt as if someone had pulled a rug out from under my feet, like I was slipping on ice. I really loved him."

As John recounts the story, he, too, looks out into the street, where a vendor pushes along his now empty hot-dog cart. "Papu immigrated to the U.S. from Latvia at the end of World War II. While I was growing up, he and my grandmother lived in the house next door, and on Saturdays in the summer he and I would always go bass fishing. I remember getting up before the sun, grabbing my fishing pole, and meeting Papu in the front seat of his well-worn Buick sedan for the drive to the fishing hole.

"While we fished, he'd sometimes get upset at how I tangled the line or baited the hook too loosely. Or whatever. But to let me know he really didn't mean it, we'd always stop on the way home at the Tasty Spot for an ice-cream cone. I'd hold my vanilla swirl cone as we sat together in the old Buick—the whole car smelling like bass—and Papu would just sit there and smile.

"Papu's death was—well, I guess you'd say it was a wake-up call for me, Clint. It reminded me how fragile life is and pressed the question for me about what lies on the other side."

"Which," Clint says, "I've gathered is a question most people don't spend enough time thinking about."

"Exactly. Life fills up fast with pressing issues. You know what that's like, I'm sure. Who has time to get eternity figured out? And yet, ultimately, what could be more important for us? Right?"

Clint shifts in his chair. "Another question," he says. "Something I'm curious about: In the way you portray what happens after we die—how much of this book is what you honestly expect eternity to be like, and how much is, well, just your imagination running wild?"

John laughs a little. "I'm not sure my imagination qualifies as wild, though I suppose I've been as curious about eternity as anyone. I've wondered if there'll be good books to read in heaven. And football games. And sex. And chocolate-chocolate-chip ice cream.

"And what about the music?" Clint asks, pointing his finger in mock seriousness.

John leans forward. "I'd guess that all the country music gets piped into hell. But as for heaven—who knows?"

Clint smiles. "Well if the request line's open, my list is long."

"Seriously though," John goes on, "even if there's a lot of specifics we can't fathom regarding eternity, there's also a lot we *can* discover, based on information we're given in the Bible.

"I just read a new book called *Heaven*. The author, a guy named Randy Alcorn, uses the Bible to show how life in heaven will be intensely dynamic—everyone busy with interesting and adventurous activities. People in heaven will be fully conscious, with actual bodies—not ghosts—and they'll eat and drink. They'll talk to and spend time with other loved ones there. The Bible even indicates there'll be animals in heaven, though I've personally had my doubts about any cats making it."

"Just don't tell that to Siegfried and Roy."

"Right. But getting back to the book, I did lean on my imagination quite a bit to depict the setting. After all, it wasn't my purpose to faithfully portray the locale up there. Who could do that? I just wanted to creatively explore the questions of *who* gets into heaven—and why. That's what I was pressing for."

"So—who *does* get in?"

"As I started writing the book, I made a mental list of the people I'd naturally expect to see in heaven. I was sure Mrs. Campbell, my second-grade teacher, would be there. Nicest person I ever met. And I figured my church's pastor, Ted Haggard, was a shoo-in. And that old lady who works at the soup kitchen downtown—she'd make it, no doubt. And Mother Teresa probably has a megamansion there, if she hasn't given it away. We can all make our lists like that, but—"

"Wait," Clint interrupts. "Gotta hear about hell, too. Who's on your reservation list for the fire and brimstone?"

John goes along. "At the top—probably terrorists and Oakland Raiders fans. Plus the guy who cut me off on I-25 this morning and told me hello in sign language.

"Seriously though, there'll probably be a lot of surprises in heaven. People thinking, *What's that guy doing here?* or *Where's so-and-so?* Fact is, here on earth we can never be fully certain in judging whether another person will make it to heaven. But the good news is that each of us *can* be fully certain about ourselves. *You* can be certain, Clint—just as much as I can."

"Come on—*absolutely* certain?"

"It's true. Through the Bible, God makes it clear that those who follow Christ—and I can tell you more about what that means—can know for certain they'll spend eternity with him."

High overhead, the sun slips behind the high, antique-brick wall next door to the patio. In the shadow, Clint lifts his sunglasses to rest on his blond hair and squints as he looks at John. "To be honest, that's where I struggle with your book. Shouldn't everyone—or at least *almost* every-one—be admitted into heaven, regardless of what they believe about Jesus?"

"Good question, Clint. And it deserves a good answer. Do you mind if I spell it out in detail?"

"Go for it, if you think you can," Clint says. "Just seems to me that the fairest and simplest approach is for practically everyone to get in."

"You're certainly not alone in that opinion. Most of us naturally think of heaven as the 'default' destiny for everyone who dies. We think we're all headed there automatically—you know, unless we've been exceptionally and horribly bad here on earth, like a mass murderer.

"But the fact is, Clint, whether we like it or not, hell is the true default destiny for all of us, including you and me. That's because, according to what the Bible teaches, each of us has a natural 'dark side,' so to speak, a sinful condition that disqualifies us from being eligible for eternal life in God's presence."

Clint interrupts. "Wait a minute. You keep taking it for granted that the Bible's true. But isn't that an awfully big assumption?"

"It doesn't have to be," John answers. "Or at least, there's more than enough evidence to support the Bible's reliability, once you fully research it. But for now—just for the sake of discussion—let's assume the Bible *is* true. When you read it, you soon discover another critical fact about our dark side: It's more offensive to God than we could possibly imagine. It earns us his intense displeasure—his 'wrath' is what the Bible calls it."

Clint frowns. "God's wrath. Reminds me of the scene where they open the ark in *Raiders of the Lost Ark*."

"And not a bad picture of it, at that. But God didn't create us with this dark side. Instead, he specifically designed each of us with the capacity for a full and open relationship with himself. That's the real reason all of us exist.

"In fact, the dark side was nonexistent in humanity until, as the Bible explains, Adam and Eve disobeyed God. Their disobedience was a catastrophe for humanity. It locked sinfulness and death into the very fabric of human nature."

Clint looks riveted, and John continues. "Ever since that time, on an individual basis, our own faults and failures and offenses—our 'sins'—have only confirmed the existence of that dark side within each of us. If we're honest about it, Clint, we have to admit that our dark side reveals itself on pretty much a daily basis. You know what I mean—the bad stuff that keeps coming up again and again.

"Think about it this way: God, who is perfectly pure and good—like the brightest, purest light—simply cannot coexist with darkness. We can't just elbow our way into his presence, like midnight pushing its way into noontime, and be accepted there as we are.

"By nature, we're all like Jack was in *The Two Doors of Heaven*—headed for a destiny in hell. The guilt for our own particular sins has earned us a 'guilty' verdict from God. And our sentence, our punishment, is this: to be kept out of his presence forever. And in eternity, that separation means hell."

Clint raises an eyebrow. "But if that's true," he argues, "there has to be something we can do about it, somehow. We can change, can't we? Can't we improve? Brighten up our dark side? Surely we aren't totally helpless."

"We all want to think so," John answers. "But that's where our inherent human sinfulness, our human weakness, comes in again. We're powerless to erase past guilt, and even if by some miracle we did, we're still incapable of preventing additional guilt in the future.

"So we're basically stuck. And we're incapable of getting unstuck on our own."

Clint isn't convinced. "But if we're all so corrupted and weak, and it's so impossible for me to correct myself, how can God hold me responsible? Why can't he understand how weak and helpless we are?"

John eagerly smiles. "That's exactly the point—he *does* fully understand our weaknesses and limitations, and that's exactly why he sent his Son Jesus to earth—to die for us, to take our punishment as our substitute.

"Maybe I could illustrate it like this: When I was seventeen, I got into a pretty bad accident while driving my father's car. It caused a lot of damage to the other guy's vehicle, and the bill was far more than I could pay at that age. I fully deserved to pay every penny, but it was beyond my ability.

"I freaked out, considering my options. One possibility was to skip my court date, try to avoid the law, and probably end up spending a while in jail. My alternative was to go to my dad, face the consequences of my bad judgment, and ask for help.

"I chose option two. To my surprise and relief, my dad paid the bill, took care of the ticket, and forgave me. Despite my overwhelming obligation, I got off free.

"That's a picture of what Jesus offers us, Clint. Our chronic darkness has wrecked our relationship with God and excluded us from heaven. The damage is done, and someone has to pay the bill. Yet we're helpless to cover it.

"That's where Jesus stepped in. He paid that bill. By

dying on the cross, he took *all* the penalty for *all* our wrong-doing—past, present, and future."

Clint looks reflective. "So that was behind what Elliott was talking about when he thought of Jesus as his 'falling star.'"

"That's it! And Jesus assures us that if we sincerely acknowledge and accept and take hold of what he did for us, we can spend our eternity with God."

Clint is still mentally wrestling. "But…I honestly see lots of obstacles to just 'accepting' this and 'acknowledging' it, to use your terms." He shakes his head. "But let's don't go into all that. Actually, I want to hear more from you about the different characters in the book—you know, their full personalities, their histories, the backstories that the book doesn't reveal. I want to make sure you've thought through each one as much as possible, because the screen-writers will want to get the full scoop from you about all of them. But why don't we take a walk around the block while we talk? I could use the exercise. Okay with you?"

Quickly agreeing, John stands and picks up his satchel, looping the strap over his shoulder.

Backstories

⫼☰

As they amble down the sidewalk, Clint slips on his sunglasses again.

"Let's take Alexis first," he says. "Sure isn't hard to see why she would have problems 'accepting' Christ, as you put it. Just look at the abuse in her past. So wrong, so unfair."

"It was, Clint. More wrong and more unjust—in God's eyes—than you or I could ever comprehend."

"So," Clint asks, "how could someone like Alexis be expected to put something so terrible out of her mind and just go along and be a good Christian?"

"God knows that it would be impossible for any of us to put that kind of pain out of our minds," John answers. "It can't be done—which is why we have to let *him* do it for us. That's exactly what Jesus makes possible for any and all of us in any situation where others have cruelly hurt us in some way.

"Listen, Clint. No one understands that kind of pain

better than Jesus. He was rejected, lied to, betrayed, then abandoned by those who had promised to defend him. His friends ditched him when the pressure hit and left him to be killed. And he went through all that to win forgiveness for you and me from God. Only in the miracle of that forgiveness can we ourselves find the ability to forgive others for their cruelty to us and to break free from it and not let it control us anymore."

Clint let out a sigh. "Then…why didn't you allow Alexis to experience that?" he asked. "Why didn't she break free?"

"We all have a choice, Clint. So did she. She made her own choice *not* to forgive and get free. Amazingly, Alexis allowed herself to live her life as a slave to her past and her pain, and it filled her with bitterness—a bitterness that blinded her. It's incredibly tragic—but that's what I see happening to her."

Clint clenches a fist. "You're saying Alexis could have just automatically gotten over the pain of being abused? Just like that?"

"No, Clint, not 'automatically.' She had to consciously consider and encounter Jesus—the reality of who he truly is, not the façade of what hypocrites like Thomas were portraying. But whenever Alexis was given that opportunity—and it happened often in her short life—she threw up intellectual objections. Things like denying the historical fact that Jesus rose from the dead, or denying the reliability of almost everything the Bible says about Jesus. Alexis was a very intelligent person, but she simply couldn't get beyond questions like that."

"But those are legitimate questions, aren't they?"

"Sure they are—sincere, legitimate questions. But the answers to them are legitimate, too. And substantial. And significant. Yet Alexis didn't sincerely search for those answers and study them. For her, throwing up the questions and leaving them unanswered was a defensive ploy. It was the way she escaped from facing the reality and ugliness of her bitterness and her own shortcomings.

"It's true it would take a miracle for Alexis to become a joyful, liberated person. But that's exactly the miracle Jesus was dying to accomplish for her. He's done it many times with people whose backgrounds were even worse than hers. There's no darkness, no pain, no mistake he can't overcome. But Alexis decided she simply wouldn't have anything to do with it.

"Ultimately, Alexis could have been just as happy a person as Millie—someone who had her own share of past hurt to deal with."

"Okay," Clint says, "tell me more about Millie. Someone in her situation—they'd have to be pretty bitter at times, wouldn't they? Maybe the book doesn't give us a fully rounded picture of her past."

"I suspect Millie had to fight against bitterness at times, absolutely," John answers. "But let me try to fill in that picture for you—at least as I see it. Millie knew Jesus personally—he was actually a daily, living presence in her life. And that's what sustained her through almost four decades of having no legs and being stuck in a wheelchair. And staying unmarried as well."

Clint cocks his head. "Wow, four decades. So how do you think Millie spent all that time?"

"Not wallowing in self-pity, that's for sure. I see her always giving herself to others, helping them however she could. Do you remember, Clint, what she was doing that day in the coffee shop?"

"Uh—yeah, I do, in fact. She was working a crossword puzzle. So how would that qualify as 'giving yourself to others'?"

"Well, Millie liked to work those puzzles with her daily coffee because it was one small way to help her keep her mind sharp. For years, Millie worked in the inner city. She taught free classes in health and baby care for several hours each week through some service programs sponsored by her church downtown. And it was a thriving, youth-oriented church, by the way—and Millie loved it. She kept up her nurse's license over the years, taking all the exams and the refresher classes. She never let up.

"Millie touched lives no matter what she did. I think some proof of that would show up at her funeral. Funerals, you know, can tell a lot about a person."

"So how did Millie's turn out?"

"Here's how I envision it going: I think her church would have been packed to overflowing, and most of the people there would have been her neighbors and friends from practically every block in the inner city. They all knew about Millie. There was plenty of crying in that church that afternoon—but there was just as much laughter and celebration. Her friends just couldn't help rejoicing over the good life she'd lived."

"You know," Clint says, "I can see having a scene in the movie that shows that. Be sure to mention all this to the screenwriters. But I gotta tell you, John—the character who fascinates me most is Elliott. What would have been the mood at the funeral for a wild guy like that?"

"In Elliott's case, I'd say the mood was mostly one of bewilderment."

"Hmm. Why would that be?"

"Do you remember what Elliott was doing on the coffee shop patio?" John asks.

"Working on his computer," Clint answers. "Oh, and singing to himself."

"Good memory. Well, ever since his experience in his BMW out on that country road a week before he died, I think Elliott had been sending personal e-mails to every acquaintance he could think of—and he had lots of them strung out across the country. He was letting them all know about his new life.

"He personalized each message, but the heart of each one was the same. He told them what happened to him on the mountain, and then what he came across at that Easter production he went to, and finally what he experienced in his car.

"In these e-mails, the climax to the story he told was always the same: He told them how, after he prayed on that rainy day, he truly felt forgiveness and how he knew that the living, risen Jesus was right there in the car with him.

"And that was an experience that stayed with him. It just so happens," John adds with a wink, "that a friend of Elliott's gave me a copy of the very last e-mail he wrote from that coffee shop."

John pulls a sheet of paper from a side pocket of his satchel, then reads aloud as they continue walking. "Near the end of the message, Elliott says this: 'I know Jesus is right here in this coffee shop with me as I write to you, Lindsay, because I know he's living inside me. There just can't be any other explanation for the change that's come over me. And I've decided I won't rest until I can talk about this with everybody I can. For the moment, that's my mission in life, and I can't wait to see what God has in store for me next.'

"Then he closes his message with this: 'I know a lot of what I'm saying probably sounds crazy to you, Lindsay, but I just want to ask you to please be patient with me. It doesn't mean I'm going to stop being your friend or anything like that. In fact, I look forward to seeing you again and talking with you in person about all of this. And I promise not to bore you (that's one thing that hasn't changed about me!) Love you, Lindsay! Later—El.'

"Then he hit 'send'—and less than a minute later, Elliott looked up to see that truck coming in their direction."

John shows the paper to Clint. In the message details at the top, the word "Sent" is followed by a date plus the time designation: "12:45 PM."

John continues. "I think that's the kind of message Elliott wrote to all his friends, to everybody he could. So when his funeral came around, Lindsay and nearly every other person in attendance had already heard the story— straight from Elliott himself—of what had happened to him and why. And most of them were as much in shock about that as they were about his dying.

"And here's something interesting: At Elliott's funeral, there was a brief talk by a high school buddy of his named Trevor—the same friend who'd invited Elliott along to the production of 'The Thorn.' Trevor knew all about what was going on in Elliott's life, and about the messages he was sending out.

"Trevor told everyone there that God had grabbed Elliott's attention big-time. Elliott had finally responded to God—just before it was too late, thankfully. Then Trevor looked out on that crowd and assured them that God was getting *their* attention, too.

"Between Trevor's appeal and Elliott's e-mails, those people came away with plenty to think about."

As the two men walk, they reach an open, brick-paved

plaza. They look around. It's mostly empty. On one side, there's an unoccupied foldout camp stool.

"Okay," Clint says, "let's move on to the professor—what was his name?"

"Sean Stafford."

"Yeah. I think I'd picture his funeral being a pretty muted occasion—unless maybe his buddies were able to hold it at the pub on a Friday night!"

"Sean would probably prefer it that way. But I'd say 'quiet' is probably an on-target description of Sean's funeral. Not much of a display of emotion. And I don't think a single person there knew anything about the midnight prayers Sean uttered inside that quiet little chapel."

Clint puts his hands in his pockets as he walks. "I remember Sean saying that he didn't know whether God even heard that prayer. *Did* God hear it? I mean—when it came time for Sean's choice to be revealed, which door do you think he went through?"

"Which one do you think, Clint?"

"Well…I thought his part in the story was a bit confusing."

"He did seem torn in opposite directions, didn't he?" John agrees. "Just like so many people who want to believe in God, but for whatever reason—social pressure maybe, cultural pressure, intellectual pressure—they can't quite commit themselves. But still, once they reach eternity, it's always either one door or the other. No in-between.

So which door do you think was Sean's choice?"

"Oh…it just isn't clear to me," Clint says. "I can't decide."

"Neither can I. Reminds me again of how none of us can judge for sure what happens to other people in eternity, but we *can* know what will happen to *us*. Kind of goes to show you—it's far better to get the truly important issues of life straightened out as early as possible, especially when it comes to eternity. Otherwise, everything gets pretty muddled."

They reach a corner and wait for a walk signal. Clint's eyes flick upward toward a massive billboard atop a brick building across the street. It's a travel agency ad showing a young couple strolling on a Caribbean beach.

"And then, of course," Clint says, "there's Jack. What more should I know about that guy?"

"Maybe you already do," John answers. "In lots of ways, I think Jack is a great deal like us. Like you and me."

"Oh, really? This I gotta hear. Explain that one for me."

On the Spot

≡

"Oh, wait," Clint says. "I bet I know what you're going to say. Jack is Everyman."

"More or less." John nods.

"So he's Mr. Average Guy. And that's why he makes you think of me! I'm flattered."

"Yeah, well, we both know there's no such thing as a person who's truly average. In different ways, we're all exceptional. Especially you and me, of course."

"Glad you added that."

"But I do see Jack in the same situation that a lot of us are in—and it can be the most dangerous place of all in terms of figuring out your eternal destiny."

"What do you mean?"

"Jack would never say his life was easy. He certainly wasn't enjoying the way his marriage was dying. But he wasn't going to let that derail his whole life. He was basically pushing forward, trying to keep all his gauges showing 'normal,' refusing to enter crisis mode. Every day for him was just more of the everyday. And when things are routine like that—which they are for most of us, most of the time—that's when it's often less likely that we consider God at all.

"That's how Jack might be a lot like you and me, Clint. For me, like so many of us, I know my life isn't all that remarkable one way or the other right now, and it could be easy to forget all about eternity. Maybe you're there, too—unless there happens to be a crisis building in your life at the moment."

Clint shrugs. "There's probably one chasing me, but I'm not looking back."

"I hear you."

They're walking at a slower pace. After a while, Clint says, "Here's a question I have about Jack. If what he went through had actually happened to someone—if they died, and experienced what Jack did, then came back to life—do you think they'd change? Or let me put it this way: If Jack's story continued on, what would happen next for him? Would he be any different?"

"Time would tell, wouldn't it? In Jack's case, I'd say he's definitely got no excuse *not* to change. But for someone with a personality like Jack's, it's going to come down to a control issue."

"How's that?"

"When it comes to our own lives, we're all control freaks, but some are that way more so than others. However, coming to Jesus and accepting his salvation means we have to let *him* be in control. That can be a very hard thing to give up. Even if we get beyond ignoring God, we're still usually resisting or resenting him.

"The truth is that God is responsible for giving us every breath, every heartbeat, and every other blessing we have, and he's constantly at work to get our attention, to reveal himself to us, and to communicate his love to us—yet most of the time we just don't see it. That darkness I talked to you about—it's so pervasive that it blinds us to the obvious. We'd rather trust in our own thought patterns and our own selfish values of happiness than to step outside our comfort zone and see the truth about how needy and empty we are. We just don't get the picture that Jesus really is our only hope."

"At the end of the book," Clint says, "Jack seemed to reach that conclusion—about his only hope, that is."

"That's right. And the proof of how real that conviction truly was would show up unmistakably in how Jack chose to live his life day by day on earth. Because earth is where everyone's true choice has to be made."

They turn another corner. They've made a full circuit and are nearing the coffee shop again.

"There's one more person in the book I wonder about," Clint says.

"Didn't we cover them all?"

"Not yet. What about Nate?"

"Oh, yes," John answers. "The lifelong thief who suddenly becomes an entry-guide to God's eternity."

Clint adds more. "You know, John, I found myself growing to like his character more and more through the story. So it was a surprise to discover what a loser he'd been in his life on earth. And then an equal surprise to see how, after all that, Nate still was guaranteed a place in heaven. Maybe this guy never did a single good thing in his whole life till he spoke a few kind words about Jesus at the end. Okay, I can see the dramatic flair in that; it works for the story. Bottom line, though—isn't it unfair?"

"Great question," John says. "One thing that's clear about this man in the Bible is that in those final hours he obviously believed the truth about Jesus—enough to reach out to Jesus as his only hope for eternity. And that's what counts. As long as we're in this world, even if we're trapped in a foxhole or fading fast on our deathbed, it's never too late to reach out to Jesus, no matter how bad we've been. Jesus really is our only hope, first and last."

The coffee shop patio is empty now, though pedestrians stream by on the sidewalk and traffic fills the street. The two men stand in the shadow of the old brick wall. Clint lifts up his sunglasses again, then leans and rests one hand on the smooth bricks. "Sometimes, though," he says, "I wonder if maybe a lot more people would embrace Christianity if only Christians didn't claim that it's the *only* way to heaven."

John nods. "Yes, but don't lose sight of the real issue. In the end, it always comes down to what Jesus says. After all, he's the one who insisted, 'I am the way, the truth, and the life. No one can come to the Father except through me.' That's what he claimed. And because Jesus is perfectly honest and perfectly loving, he tells us the truth about that for our own sake.

"From a certain narrow human perspective, his words might look overly exclusive—maybe you'd say religiously chauvinistic. But Jesus was simply explaining reality to us for our own good. And his words are totally *in*clusive, not *ex*clusive—his invitation is for absolutely everyone. Including me and you."

Clint grins. "Me? Are you putting me on the spot? Where's that fake twenty-dollar bill?"

"Forget the twenty-dollar bill. I'm serious. After all, your eternal destiny is at stake, Clint. It's something you want to take care of as soon as possible, while you can—and not wait, for example, until after some runaway truck slams into our patio here."

"Heaven forbid."

"Right."

"So, John, what exactly would I do—to take care of it if I felt I needed to?"

"It comes down to simply *believing*. That's what you have to do. Yeah—I know: Sounds too simple. But it's true. Belief is the only requirement. Do you remember the Bible verse little Millie recited as she and her parents gathered around their scrawny Christmas tree?"

"Whoa, that's asking a lot. The Bible and I haven't exactly been on speaking terms. But, if I recall…I think it was something like…uh…'God loves the world…uhh…'"

"Good start! This was it: 'For God so loved the world, that He gave His only Son, that whoever *believes* in Him should not perish, but have everlasting life.' It means that everyone who enters heaven will get there the same way—through Jesus.

"It also means that everyone in the whole world is welcome in heaven, regardless of past mistakes or current circumstances, as long as they believe in Jesus. On their own, no one can be good enough to get into heaven, but no one can be too bad *not* to get in either. The people who make it into heaven aren't good people or bad people, but *forgiven people*. That's the bottom line—believing in Christ by accepting the forgiveness he freely offers.

"And when you have that belief, that faith, then the first person to acknowledge it to is God himself. You do that by talking to God—praying. You can tell him something like this. I'll write the words down for you, so you can take them with you."

John pulls up a chair at the table nearest the wall and removes a yellow pad from his satchel. He writes out these words, then reads them aloud as Clint looks over his shoulder.

"Lord God, forgive me for living my life for myself.

"I realize there's nothing I can do to earn my salvation from hell and to gain eternal life with you. Jesus is my only hope.

"Thank you for sending your Son to die in my place and to pay the penalty for my sins. Thank you for never giving up on me and for giving me what I don't deserve.

"Today, I accept Jesus as my Savior. I surrender my life to him and I put my faith in him.

"That's it." John rips the sheet from the pad and hands it to Clint, who stares at the words.

"If you, or anyone, sincerely prays that prayer, Clint—or something like it—you can be assured you'll spend eternity in heaven with God. Your choice will be made."

Suddenly, both men are startled by a screech of rubber on pavement. On the street immediately in front of them, a truck has nearly slammed into a swerving bicyclist. The biker yells. The driver shouts back.

Clint is tense. He sits down at the table across from John and touches his fingers to his forehead. He looks again at the sheet of paper on the table.

"Pray this prayer from your heart," John explains again, "and you'll be sure. You'll never have any doubt again… about those two doors in heaven."

• • •

I hope you've thought carefully about
the brief prayer written out for Clint.
If after reading this book, you have prayed
this prayer for the first time and would
like information about the next steps,
please visit www.twodoorsofheaven.com.
At this website you can also find answers
to additional questions
you may have about finding
salvation in Jesus Christ.

—*John Bolin*

A Discussion Guide

—

for

The Two Doors
of Heaven

Discussion Guide

≡

Use this guide to more fully enjoy reading *The Two Doors of Heaven* with a friend or in a group.

Part I—To the Doors

1. For the chapter entitled "Lunch Break"

1. What kind of person is Jack Gates? How does he come across to you? What would seem to be his personality strengths and weaknesses?

2. Put yourself in Jack's shoes for a moment. What important choices has he apparently made in life to bring about his current circumstances?

3. Do you sense that Jack made a mistake by not becoming an artist? Why or why not? How might life have been different for him?

2. For the chapter entitled "Last Words"

1. From the limited evidence you see here, how would you describe Jack and Sydney's relationship? If you were a marriage counselor, what suggestions would you make to Jack at this point in his life?

2. How would you describe Jack's relationship with his children?

3. What are the most interesting things you learn in this chapter about (a) the woman in the wheelchair? (b) the young man wearing flip-flops? (c) the woman named Alexis? (d) the professor who's with Alexis?

3. For the chapter entitled "Floating"

1. Is Jack experiencing reality here, or just a terrible dream? Why do you think so?

2. How would you summarize the initial reaction of each character here—Jack, Elliott, Alexis, the professor, and Millie—to being in an after-death state? Which person's reaction is closest to what you'd expect your own reaction to be in such a situation?

3. At this point in the story, which character do you most enjoy? Which one would you most like to spend more time with?

4. Which character are you least attracted to here?

5. Which character do you think is most like you?

4. For the chapter entitled "A Journey Begins"

1. Have you ever met anyone like Nate? How would you describe his personality? What guesses could you make about his background?

2. Think about Jack's childhood perspective on death as he reveals it in this chapter. How similar is it to your own thoughts about this subject?

3. As Nate led the little band of travelers into the unknown of eternity, he turned around at one point to ask them, "What did you expect?" How would you answer that question? What are your own expectations about eternity?

4. Nate defines eternal life as being "never, even for a moment, anything less than this: living with the infinite One who gives unending joy and pleasure in his presence." What do you think of that description? How appealing does it sound?

5. As they discussed their expectations of eternity, the travelers mention reincarnation, ghosts, and even being changed into an energy force. What are your own views on those topics as they relate to our existence after death?

5. For the chapter entitled "Farther In and Higher Up"

1. What, if anything, was a surprise to you in this chapter?

2. Jack wonders what "being in God's presence" would be like. What do you think it would be like?

3. Nate tells Jack, "Being in his presence is what God created you for...on earth as well as in eternity." How do you respond to that statement? Should that be our purpose in life? Why or why not?

4. Why do you think Alexis hates being where she is so much?

6. For the chapter entitled "Millie"

1. From the limited evidence given in this chapter, how would you summarize Millie's childhood? In view of her circumstances, how happy do you think she was? What would you say was the best thing about her childhood?

2. After Jack saw how Millie was injured in Vietnam, he quickly felt shame and regret for how he'd ignored her in the coffee shop. Why did he feel this way? Jack thought of that incident in the coffee shop as "the truest revelation of his character, the unmistakable picture of what kind of person he actually was." Do you think this assessment is correct?

3. Alexis said about Millie, "I can be happy for her." Do you think Alexis was speaking honestly?

4. How do you respond to Millie's character?

7. For the chapter entitled "Alexis"

1. From the brief glimpse in this chapter, how would you summarize the childhood Alexis experienced?

2. What was your emotional reaction to the way Thomas treated Alexis? What thoughts came to you?

3. Alexis told the professor, "God is only who we make him to be. It doesn't matter how we worship or whom we worship or even *if* we worship." To what extent do you agree with her about this? How free are we to decide individually how to relate to God?

4. In defending her choice to reject God, Alexis said, "I have nothing to be ashamed of. I have no regrets. There was no way I could have made any other decision." Do you think she was right about that? Did she have any other choices?

5. How do you respond to the character of Alexis?

8. For the chapter entitled "The Professor"

1. In his philosophy class, Professor Stafford asked his students, "Isn't that basically what we've done in our culture? Haven't we murdered God?" If you were in that classroom that day, how would you answer that question?

2. Speaking with his academic colleagues in the pub about the philosopher Kierkegaard, Professor Stafford said, "The choice of faith isn't a real choice. It's something we make up out of despair—a leap in the dark with nothing to land on." To what extent do you agree with that description of faith?

3. Were you surprised at all to hear what the professor prayed in the candlelit chapel? What does that incident reveal about his character?

4. The professor later wondered if his prayer in the chapel was "real enough for God." Do you think it was? Why or why not?

5. How do you respond to the professor's character?

9. For the chapter entitled "Elliott"

1. How do you respond to Elliott's character?

2. Elliott seemed to have everything a person could want. Yet he said, "It's nothing when you've got a hole inside you, and everything you frantically cram into it just drains out faster and faster, leaving you emptier than ever." What exactly was that "hole" inside Elliott? Do you think that same hole is in all of us? Why or why not?

3. As Elliott edged his body toward the mountain cliff, he was thinking, *I knew that dying was no worse than I deserved.* Do you think this was an accurate appraisal of Elliott's worth? Why or why not?

4. What was the "miracle" that Elliott said he experienced? How would you describe that miracle in your own words?

5. Elliott spoke of Jesus as "my falling star." What do you think he meant by that?

10. For the chapter entitled "Jack"

1. What significant pieces of information do you learn about Jack in this chapter? What fuller picture do you gain of his personality and of his strengths and weaknesses?

2. From the limited evidence in this chapter, how would you summarize the childhood Jack experienced?

3. What more do you learn here about Jack and Sydney's relationship? What more do you learn about Jack's relationship with his children?

4. At this point in Jack's experience, what is it he wants most?

5. Jack described himself in this chapter as feeling "beaten up." Why was that? Was it right for him to feel this way?

6. Nate spoke of the choices that would determine whether Jack would ever see his wife again. What might these choices be?

7. Nate reminded Jack of the many good experiences he'd enjoyed in life, asking him "whether all this was more than you deserved and whether it was more than you ever took the trouble to thank God for." What do you think Jack's answers should have been to these questions? And what would be *your* answers if those same questions were asked of you?

11. For the chapter entitled "Nate"

1. What, if anything, was a surprise to you in this chapter?

2. How do you respond to Nate's character?

3. From the limited evidence provided in this chapter, how would you summarize the childhood Nate experienced?

4. What do you think was Nathan's motive behind the request he made to Jesus on the cross? What did that question reveal about this hardened criminal's heart at that time?

5. How did Jesus respond to Nathan's request? Why do you think this response was so surprising to Nate?

6. As he neared death on the cross, Jesus cried out to God, "Why have you forsaken me?" What did he mean by that?

7. In Jack's experiences so far in eternity, what do you think are the most important lessons he has learned? Do you think Jack is changing?

12. For the chapter entitled "Two Doors"

1. In his thoughts at this moment, Jack decided that failing to accept Jesus "was the same as rejecting him." What led Jack to such a conclusion?

2. How would you summarize Jack's impression of the hell that apparently awaits him?

3. Why was it now too late for Jack to "choose Jesus"?

13. For the chapter entitled "Movie Man"

1. How do you respond to Clint's character?

2. How does the author, John Bolin, describe his childhood?

3. What questions does this chapter raise in your mind?

4. Clint asks John, "Shouldn't everyone—or at least *almost* everyone—be admitted into heaven, regardless of what they believe about Jesus?" How would you summarize the answer John gave him?

5. John refers to a "dark side" in each one of us. How would you describe that dark side in your own words? And what has God done about that problem, according to John's explanation?

14. For the chapter entitled "Backstories"

1. John and Clint discuss a number of funerals in this chapter. What would you expect *your* funeral to be like? What words do you think would describe it?

2. Think again of each of the four characters discussed in this chapter—Alexis, Millie, Elliott, and the professor. How would you summarize the way each of them responded to God in his or her life?

3. What questions does this chapter raise in your mind?

15. For the chapter entitled "On the Spot"

1. John mentions that it can sometimes be "dangerous" to be living a fairly routine life. In John's opinion, why is that so?

2. "When it comes to our own lives," John says, "we're all control freaks." Do you agree with that assessment? Why or why not? Why is it difficult for us to yield control of our lives to God?

3. When Clint mentions the "exclusiveness" of Christianity, John responds by saying, "Don't lose sight of the real issue. In the end, it always comes down to what Jesus says." How exactly is Jesus the "real issue"?

4. According to John's explanation, what does it mean to "believe" in Jesus?

5. What is your response to the prayer that John writes out for Clint? Is this a prayer you would like to pray at this time for your own life and eternal future?